THE
PURPLE
HEART

MARC TALBERT is the author of many ac-
claimed novels for young readers, including *Dead
Birds Singing* and *Pillow of Clouds*. He lives in
Tesuque, New Mexico.

THE
PURPLE
HEART

MARC TALBERT

AN AVON  CAMELOT BOOK

AVON BOOKS
A division of
The Hearst Corporation
1350 Avenue of the Americas
New York, New York 10019

First Avon Camelot Printing: November 1993

CAMELOT TRADEMARK REG. U.S. PAT. OFF. AND IN OTHER COUNTRIES, MARCA REGISTRADA, HECHO EN U.S.A.

Printed in the U.S.A.

OPM   10 9 8 7 6 5 4 3 2 1

For
Captain Thomas Avey, USMC,
brother and friend
and
Edward A. Knapp,
friend and patron of science and art.

Spring 1967

CHAPTER

1

Luke couldn't sleep. He'd kicked off his covers, but he was still sweating. Luke never wore pajamas if he could help it. But tonight he'd worn them to bed in case a tornado was sighted and the town's sirens went off and he had to rush down to the safety of the basement. He didn't want to be naked if the house collapsed and rescue workers had to dig through the debris to save him and his picture was in the newspaper, on the front page.

Even so, he hated wearing pajamas. Tonight they clung to him like waxed paper left out in the sun. "Crud!" he mumbled, enjoying the way his father's favorite word scuffed along the back of his tongue. He lay as quietly as he could— spread-eagled, eyes closed—and tried to imagine himself floating on a layer of cool air.

Tornado season had come in May, a month early, with its greenish dusks in the middle of the day and its eerie stillness before storms. Luke wondered if a storm was approaching or if the night was simply breathless. Within the past week, Luke and his mother had spent three

3

nights in the basement, staring wide-eyed at the floor joists above them, counting the nails that held them, praying that the boards would stay together. Luke and his mother had been in sleeping bags that they'd unrolled against the base of the cinder-block walls, their feet far apart and their heads almost bumping together in the southwest corner, close enough to share the light of a candle nubbin and hold hands across the clammy basement floor.

It should have been a treat to sleep in the cool of the basement, camping out with his mother, surrounded by an emergency stash of water, soda, crackers, peanut candies, extra candles, and plenty of matches. But sleeping in the basement meant that tornados or violent storms raged above, threatening to smash their house and everything in it.

Luke's fear and hatred of tornados was growing stronger all the time. He'd seen countless photos in the newspaper of smashed buildings and heard scores of stories about lengths of straw driven through trees, mobile homes turned on their heads, and horses carried for miles and laid gently on the ground, unscratched but dead. Luckily, the town of Clifton nestled in a wide valley created by two converging rivers, and so far tornados had always skipped from valley rim to valley rim, jumping over the town, never touching down. But several times in the past couple of years Luke had seen twisting, blurry, spinning tubes descend from the sky, not quite reaching the tops of trees, seeming like loose, wobbly,

4

high-powered drills almost free of their bits, dangerous and unpredictable, whining and poking through boiling clouds the color of diesel exhaust.

Shuddering, Luke opened his eyes and looked out his bedroom window. Heat lightning flashed at irregular moments, not streaking down in crackling shafts but coming from beyond the horizon, as if the surrounding towns were being bombed by enemy troops or grain elevators were being blown up by roving bands of enemy guerrillas. Thunder followed each flash, faint and low, more a feeling than a sound, each time making Luke think that his ears were stuffed up. He stared at the patches of dim stars that barely shone through dark blotches of leaves of the ancient apple tree that grew outside his bedroom window. They disappeared with the heat lightning and reappeared moments before the thunder.

In his mind he heard his father's voice, brave and sure, the way he imagined him during combat: *We need mortar cover on Hill 33! Charlie is moving in . . . fast! More mortar! Alpha Company under attack! Get a move on! Get dancing 'fore the music stops! Don't waltz! Get Rocking 'n Rolling!*

Although he knew that his father couldn't make tornados go away or keep the house from flying apart, Luke remembered feeling safe before his father had left for Vietnam. But his father had returned home yesterday and Luke felt as unsafe in violent weather as he had when he and his mother were alone.

Sitting partway up, he reached above his

5

shoulders, flipped over the pillow, and let his head sink into the fresh coolness of its newly exposed side. Closing his eyes, he tried to will himself asleep. But each time he heard the low rumble in the distance, he expected to feel the air shift, to feel it drop heavily to the ground and then silently bounce upward as a storm approached. And then his imagination took over and the thunder grew in his head, sounding like houses exploding or bullet-riddled, shrapnel-shredded barns collapsing, or mines popping off—sounds his father must have heard every day in Vietnam. Luke was certain that his father had been brave enough not to let these sounds bother him any more than the noise of a train in the distance. He wished he were as brave as his father.

Flipping onto his side, facing away from the window, Luke folded the pillow over his head so that it covered both ears. He could no longer hear the thunder but, in the silence he'd created, unwelcome images jarred his thoughts.

He saw her so clearly that she could have been standing in front of him: his mother, pregnant, her belly swelled to an enormous size, smiling from the kitchen door as he came home from school over a month ago. She'd hugged him so tightly Luke had been afraid her belly would split. And then she'd held him at arm's length—his belly button almost even with hers, almost

6

down the plane's rolling stairs and stepping onto the tarmac.

And then one figure caught his eye. Luke had squinted. This man was bent over sideways from the weight of the duffel bag hanging from a shoulder—he walked old, taking baby steps, as if something were wrong with his feet or his legs. One hand clutched a cane. But the closer he got, the faster Luke's heart beat.

His father had hobbled toward Luke and his mother and, to Luke's surprise, stopped a good ten or fifteen feet in front of them, far enough away so Luke could barely read "Canvin" in the squared letters on the plastic name tag pinned above the uniform's breast pocket. Luke looked up and saw his father's mouth quiver and read confusion in his eyes. Letting the duffel bag slide off his shoulder and drop to his feet, he looked from Luke to Luke's mother and back again, as if he couldn't believe what he saw.

His father's face reminded Luke of that of a kid who'd just scraped his knee and didn't know whether to cry or not. Finding his father's eyes too painful to look at, Luke lowered his gaze.

And then he heard his mother gasp and cry, "Patrick!" as she rushed toward his father. Luke saw his father wince as he bent over at the waist, his hips pushed away from Luke's mother by her stomach but his chin hooked over her shoulder. And then Luke saw his father's eyes close as his arms reached around his wife's shoulders. The cane clattered onto the tarmac.

As Luke watched, his father's face pulled itself

9

into a knot, gathering itself around his puckered mouth. Tears slicked down his cheeks and snot dripped from his nose. And then came the tortured sound of a winded horse—hollow and deep—as his father's mouth opened.

Luke wouldn't have been more shocked if the airplane behind his father had suddenly fallen apart piece by piece. He'd never seen his father cry before. Luke dropped his eyes again, this time staring at the scuffed tips of his dress shoes—shocked and ashamed.

He didn't know what to do or think or feel. Standing stock-still, he waited until his father and mother had stopped crying. Only then did he step forward, almost stepping up to his father—suddenly wanting to hug him—but at the last moment chickening out, veering away and picking up the duffel bag and cane at his feet.

He jumped as his father patted him on the back. "Luke, you've grown," he said in a choked and wavering voice. "Are . . . are you shaving yet?"

Luke knew that his father was trying to joke around, but the rough way his father then rubbed the top of his head with a row of knuckles took all the fun out of it. Luke hated having his head rubbed, and his father knew it. Maybe, Luke thought, he's so tired that he's forgotten.

He'd walked behind them—behind his father, who leaned on his mother for support—struggling as much with his feelings as with the heavy bag whose strap cut into his shoulder. His scalp crawled where his father had rubbed it.

★

"Crud," Luke mumbled to himself, wishing he wasn't remembering any of this. The way it should have been was so different. There should have been a brass band playing as his father walked down the rolling stairs, keeping time with his firm, measured steps. A cloud of balloons should have lifted from behind the airplane as he reached the tarmac, filling the sky with shrinking polka dots of red, white, and dark, dark blue. And as his father strode toward the fence, the sun should have sparkled from the rows of medals pinned to his chest, clanging bell-like against each other as they swaggered back and forth.

But it hadn't happened that way at all. It had happened so differently, so miserably.

Luke sat up in his bed, letting the pillow fall backward onto the mattress. The ride from Des Moines had been quiet and his mother had driven—he couldn't remember another time when his mother had driven when his father was in the car. When they got home, his father, moving as if he were underwater and refusing any help, had hung up his uniform and jammed the cane and the contents of his duffel bag into a footlocker that Luke helped him drag from the basement to the hall closet. After that he'd choked down a sandwich, given Luke and his mother clumsy hugs, gone to bed, and slept through last night and most of today.

Luke stared out the window at the lightning, feeling queasy from remembering these things

11

and from being so hot and sticky and being unable to sleep. Deciding that perhaps a little milk would calm his stomach and help him fall asleep, Luke slipped off the bed and quietly eased into the hallway. He went by memory rather than by sight in the hall's stifling darkness and almost ran into the opened door of the hallway closet. Stepping sideways just in time to avoid banging his head, Luke stopped and stared.

His father was kneeling on the hallway floor in his pajamas, probing his footlocker with the fading beam of a small flashlight. Medals and hats and boots and half-folded clothes sprawled on the floor beside him. Dog tags hung from a chain around his father's neck. There seemed to be too many of them.

"Huh?" his father grunted, shining the light into Luke's face, blinding him for a moment. "Oh," he said, sounding relieved as he lowered the flashlight's beam. Luke blinked away the blindness. His father looked embarrassed, as if he'd been caught stealing.

"Hi," Luke said softly, not knowing what else to say.

"What're you doing up so late?" his father asked, an unguarded gruffness in his voice.

"I . . . I couldn't sleep," Luke whispered, overcome by shyness. "I . . . I was going to get a glass of milk . . . to help me . . ."

His father's face softened as he considered Luke's answer. "It's hotter than a Saigon . . . lady," he finally said, his voice gentler than before. "Couldn't sleep, either. Seems that . . ." He

12

closed his mouth and his eyes narrowed, as if in pain. "The thunder and lightning were . . . spooking me."

His father, afraid of the thunder and lightning? Naw! he thought. But his father did almost look scared, and Luke dropped his gaze to the littered floor. One medal caught his eye. It was purple and shaped like a heart. It was frightening and beautiful at the same time. In the darkened hallway, the golden profile of George Washington burned into the purple, almost seeming to glow. A Purple Heart? Luke had heard of them before, but he'd never seen one. *The* Purple Heart, awarded for wounds in battle?

"Is that . . . is that a Purple Heart?" he asked, pointing as he knelt.

He looked up after a few moments, surprised that his father didn't answer, wondering if his father had heard him.

His father had heard him, all right. And what Luke saw made him wish he'd never asked. His father had never looked at him like that before, and in the deep shadows cast by the flashlight he saw a strangeness in his father's eyes that he didn't recognize, an anger that was chilling.

"Yeah. It's a Purple Heart," said his father, grimacing. "They gave it to me after I was wounded . . . gave it to me in the hospital." His father reached out and touched the medal. "Crud," he muttered. Suddenly he grabbed it and threw it into the footlocker. With quick, choppy movements he grabbed a boot and threw it in also.

13

"Better get myself back to bed . . . before your ma wakes up," his father said, not looking at Luke. "Won't be any good in the morning if I don't. Won't be any good . . . at all."

"I . . . I'll just . . . I'll . . ." Luke stammered as he stepped around his father, keeping his back to the darkness, facing his father but not looking at his face.

He rushed to the kitchen and slopped milk into a glass, drinking it so fast that each gulp choked down his throat like a handful of marbles. He was glad now that he'd worn pajamas tonight. His father had been like a stranger, and Luke would have felt embarrassed with nothing on.

Cautiously, he walked back to the hall. His father was gone and everything was back in the closet.

What's going on?

Numb, Luke crawled into bed, finally falling asleep to that question repeating itself over and over, echoing the sound of distant thunder.

CHAPTER

2

Luke ran, leaning into every turn, hunched over and holding a textbook like a rifle against his chest. Feeling a breeze through his hair, he ducked and made a few low *chunka-chunka* sounds, pretending to sprint under the slow-moving blades of an idling helicopter.

Lifting his head—luckily, he remembered he was out in the open now, away from the drooping blades that carved a flattened umbrella shape in the air—he took a deep breath and sped up. He wanted to be home ... now. After his restless night, Luke had felt tired all day. Finally school was over and he hadn't even stopped by Mike's house—he'd just yelled "Good-bye!" and kept on running as he passed Mike's driveway.

"Hey! Where ya going?" Mike had bellowed. He'd sounded surprised and maybe even a bit hurt. Luke almost always messed around with him after school, playing war games or watching television.

"Home!" Luke called over his shoulder. "See you tomorrow!"

That morning he'd waited and waited until the

last possible minute, but he'd had to leave for school before his father got up. All day long he wished he'd seen his father sitting at the table wearing his battered construction worker's hard hat—the hat that perched on his head and jiggled every time he took a sip of coffee, jiggled as if it were delicately balanced on an egg that he'd hidden underneath. All day long Luke wished he'd seen his father that morning, all rested up and back to his old self. And now he wished he could run even faster—he wished he could *fly!*—so that he could be with his father at this very moment.

Luke had spent the whole school day remembering his father before he went off to Vietnam. He remembered his square face and the way his blue eyes twinkled and that his ears seemed to fold back, lying closer to his head, when he laughed. He remembered his father's thick arms, muscles bulging as he lifted his coffee cup, tense with being careful of such a tiny thing.

And, fidgeting at his desk, Luke remembered how much his father loved to tell stories, sitting on the edge of his bed with hair still stiff from cement dust and lime. And Luke remembered his father's hands, the skin fitting over his finger bones like mud-crusted garden gloves, rough from handling bricks and cement blocks in the heat of summer and the cold of winter, his fingernails thick and yellow as a horse's teeth.

When Luke realized that he couldn't remember any of his father's stories, he felt almost sick with despair. He'd strained to remember, staring at his math book, allowing the numbers to leapfrog

16

over each other, to race toward the equal sign whether or not they were correct.

But it was no use. All he could remember was that his father's stories were funny and that he could make Luke laugh until it hurt and that then he would laugh, too, at his own cleverness. And Luke remembered the sweet smell of beer on his father's breath, almost as sweet as bread baking.

Luke rounded the last corner and charged down the sidewalk that led to the front of his house. Rushing up to the driveway, he slid to a stop and, suddenly shy, walked toward the kitchen door. What if his father was the way he'd been last night? What if he wasn't back to his old self? These questions exploded in his head as he walked to the kitchen door, each step heavier than the last. Luke wasn't sure he wanted to find out the answers.

The door opened just as he reached for the handle, and his mother beckoned him inside, a shushing finger to her lips. Luke followed her.

"Your dad's napping," she whispered, and then she gestured toward the kitchen table, on which sat a plate of chocolate-chip cookies. "I'll get you some milk."

Luke sat in his usual chair, placed his book on the table, and watched his mother pour a glass of milk and bring it over. She was wearing a long, loose, mud-colored maternity dress, which fell around her legs like a sun-faded curtain. It made her feet seem as if they had nothing to do with the way her stomach moved from side to side as

17

she walked toward the table. The top part of her appeared to float, carrying the dress with it, and her feet seemed barely able to keep up.

She sat opposite him and stretched out her legs, her feet pointing toward the center of the kitchen. She rested her hands on the hill of her stomach, her finger tips touching. "Luke," she said, "I'd like for you to be especially quiet around the house for the next couple of weeks or so. Your father needs a lot of rest . . . a lot of peace and quiet." She tilted her head to one side and studied him.

Luke swallowed and his stomach filled with disappointment.

"With the baby coming and all . . . well, it's gonna be rough for a while, Luke," she continued, sitting up in her chair and reaching over the table toward his hands. "Babies take a lot of work . . . at least new babies do, and . . . and we'll be real short on sleep for a while. Your dad needs to get rested up before all that happens. I hope you understand . . . and I just know you'll do what you can to help, honey . . . so your father can get back on his feet. . . ."

She leaned into her chair, her face longer than usual. "Do you understand, Luke?"

"Sure," he said, so softly he could barely hear himself. "I understand." He understood that his father wasn't back to his old self after all, that his father was still the way he'd been last night. He understood that everything was messed up and that nothing was going to get better anytime soon.

Luke stuffed the rest of the cookie into his mouth. "I've got homework," he mumbled through the crumbs, getting up from the table and grabbing his book.

★

Luke sat on his bed, looking out his window at the gnarled limbs of the old apple tree. He'd half expected his mother to call after him, asking him to come back into the kitchen so that she could find out about his day. She hadn't. Maybe she hadn't because she was trying to be as quiet as possible. Maybe she hadn't because she had other things to do that were more important—like seeing if his father was all right. Maybe she hadn't called after him because she understood that he needed to be alone. But no—it seemed as if his mother could think only of his father and of the baby that had taken over her body and their lives.

He held his breath and listened. The house was too quiet. It was like the quiet before a thunderstorm, before hail danced like popping corn on the lawn.

Luke sat in his bedroom for a long time, thinking and staring, trying not to feel his growing disappointment, sharp as hunger pains. He listened for any sounds of movement in the house. There were none. As he sat, he thought of his father getting off the plane and of his father in the hallway last night. His thoughts kept returning to the Purple Heart, its image burned

19

into his mind, along with the way his father had thrown it into the footlocker.

And he thought of the questions Mike had asked him as they walked to school that morning.

"How many gooks did your dad kill?" Mike had asked, as if Luke and his father had been up all night talking about the war like best buddies. And then before he'd had a chance to answer, Mike fired another question at him. "Did he see their brains splatter?"

Mike's questions bothered him. He'd barely seen his father since yesterday. He didn't even know how his father had been wounded. But Mike would have been disappointed to hear that, so Luke made up answers. "He killed two hundred gooks . . . you know, give or take." Mike didn't seem satisfied with this answer. "Sure he saw brains splatter . . . and guts and blood . . . and teeth, too." Mike had looked a little more satisfied, but not very.

Luke sat in his bedroom long enough so that the shadows of the apple tree outside had shifted noticeably, reminding him that it might almost be time for the television news to start. Maybe it already had.

Before his father had gone off to Vietnam, Luke had never really watched the television news. It had bored him. But for several months now, he'd been a television news fanatic.

Luke never admitted this to anybody, but the reason he'd never missed a night of news was because he secretly hoped to see his father talking to Morley Safer or some other hotshot reporter, telling them about a particularly brave thing that he'd done or a successful campaign that he'd just led.

Now, even with his father home, he craved the news. Luke got up off the bed and walked to his door, listened for a moment, and heard nothing. Being as quiet as possible, he walked out into the hallway—keeping close to the wall and its shadow—and then into the living room. He looked around. It was empty. He dropped to his knees in front of the television, turned the tiny knob on the far right of the set, and sat within an arm's length of the screen so that he could hear without turning the volume up above a murmur.

It took a while for the television set to warm up. As the screen grew brighter—an approaching headlight shining through a thick fog—Walter Cronkite's matter-of-fact voice became audible. And then a ghostly image appeared, flickering and growing stronger. As the screen's fog cleared, Luke saw Walter Cronkite in front of a large map of Vietnam that bent neatly around the curve of his head and down toward his shoulder. Luke had often marveled at how Vietnam fitted Walter Cronkite's shoulder.

These days, the Vietnam War was always the first thing on the news, and Luke was late but not too late.

". . . past nine days, an estimated eight thousand North Vietnamese Regulars have tried to capture a key outpost that straddles a major enemy infiltration supply route to Da Nang,"

21

Walter Cronkite said, looking down as he shifted the top paper in his hands to the bottom of the stack. Looking up, he continued, almost smiling. "That siege finally ended today, but Allied soldiers pushing out from the base to secure the surrounding area found no trace of the enemy. Allied commanders now believe that the enemy troops have pulled back, possibly behind the border in Laos, to regroup for further attacks. We have a report today from Richard Threlkeld."

The screen seemed to blink, and Luke heard the *chunka-chunka* sound of helicopters before the next scene materialized: Men were rushing away from several helicopters through tall grass, hunched over and cradling rifles in their arms. It was then that he heard a loud moan coming from the doorway behind him. "In the aftermath of the siege, Allied soldiers have begun a mop-up campaign. . . ." Richard Threlkeld's urgent voice overpowered the sound of the helicopters as Luke's head snapped sideways to see what had made the moaning sound.

The light of the television flickered, making his father's face look as if it were twitching. Stubble softened his father's chin, and deep tired lines rumpled his cheeks. His father listed to one side, leaning against the side of the couch, his left hand gripping its back as if he were about to lose his balance.

"Dad . . ." Luke pushed himself up with his hands, swinging his knees under him and twisting around at the same time. He was certain that

22

his father hadn't been there when he had crept into the living room.

". . . and according to field commanders these troops, walking in elephant grass taller than a man, encountered frequent signs of the enemy, but had little contact with them."

His father grimaced, not taking his eyes off the television, and Luke glanced at the screen to see what was the matter. There was a helmeted soldier, hunched under the weight of a plump backpack, pushing aside enormous blades of grass with the barrel of his rifle.

The scene suddenly flashed to a village, houses with thatched roofs and short peasants wearing loose pajama-like outfits and hats that looked like miniatures of the roofs. The peasants seemed bewildered as American soldiers lumbered around. Richard Threlkeld's voice droned on.

Luke had seen it all so many times before. Looking up, he saw that his father was staring at the screen as if Luke wasn't even in the room. His mouth was pulled back into a grimace and his teeth were bared, his eyes squinched tight.

Suddenly, Luke heard Walter Cronkite's voice again. "In the nation's capital, more than a dozen students were arrested today for burning draft cards on the steps of the Lincoln Memorial, protesting the war in Vietnam."

His father groaned again, louder this time, pain crumpling his face. He stood, covering his face with both hands, his shoulders shaking soundlessly, wagging his head back and forth.

Terrified, Luke spun on his heels and reached

23

for the far right-hand knob on the television. His hand froze when he saw what was there.

Three shaggy-haired young men—hippies, his father had always called them, as if it were a dirty word—were being dragged down some white steps by policemen. One of them was shouting, "I will not burn women and children! I will not kill for my country!" *Coward,* Luke thought, wrenching the knob, killing the television screen. It was the worst insult he could think of.

Turning around, Luke faced the couch.

His father was no longer there.

CHAPTER

3

That night Luke crept down the hallway, clothed only in darkness, having finally discarded his pajamas in the unbearable heat. His stomach felt like a helium-filled balloon rising in his gut, shoving his heart and lungs aside. And his head seemed to shrink to the size of a pinhead. The pin's point was aimed at the rising balloon.

To clear his mind, Luke pretended he was a member of the Green Beret Special Forces, slinking through the jungles in search of Vietcong camps or trails. Mindful of booby traps, he felt the floor with his toes before he placed weight on his advancing foot—rocking backward from the ball behind his toes to the plumpness of his heels. Keeping watch, his head bobbed back and forth, his ears tuned to any kind of noise from the far end of the hall.

It was late, well past midnight. The last noise he'd heard from his parents' bedroom had been a couple of hours ago: deep, muffled cries followed by comforting sounds from his mother mingling with long, low sobs. A cry from his father had wakened Luke—he didn't know at first what it was—and had scared him more than anything he could remember. Goose bumps spread, rippling over his body. It had never occurred to him that his father might have nightmares. But what else could the bellowing and the choked cries and the sobs have been?

Luke paused in the hallway, waiting for his feelings to catch up with him. Ten minutes ago he'd been lying on his back, awake and feeling as naked inside as he was on the outside. He'd stared at the ceiling of his bedroom wondering what could have been chasing his father in his father's dream, or what dark and endless hole his father had been falling into. And then he'd stared out his window, at the dark blobs of leaves on the apple tree. No stars shone tonight. A layer of woolly clouds blanketed the sky, keeping in the heat soaked up by the earth during the day, sealing in moisture—thick as breath trapped in a sleeping bag.

As he lay awake, an image grew until it controlled his thoughts. It was as if the Purple Heart were pinned to the inside of his forehead, swinging from eye to eye, swinging so that he couldn't avoid seeing it no matter how much he struggled to look elsewhere. As it swung, it shimmered, just as it had when Luke had first seen it in the hallway, floating in the shallow pool of light.

Could the Purple Heart hold answers to the questions he'd hoped to ask his father? Luke couldn't shake the feeling that, maybe, to hold the Purple Heart was to hold the answers to why his father walked with a limp and why his father cried out in the night. Maybe.

Stopping in front of the hall closet, Luke crouched, listening with his entire body, each hair on his head tingling and alert. Carefully, he grasped the doorknob, twisting and pulling at the same time, slipped inside, and closed the door behind him.

It was as if he'd completely disappeared, melted into the darkness with the texture of coats and the smell of rubber boots. He closed his eyes, and for an instant the undersides of his eyelids seemed brighter than the closet's darkness. He wondered if the baby closed up inside his mother felt like this.

He groped in front of his shins, and his fingertips seemed to buzz as they touched the hard front edge of the footlocker. Easing down onto his knees and resting his bottom on the chilly callus of his heels, Luke carefully lifted the lid, releasing musty air. He felt the floor next to him and found a rubber boot to jam into the hinge of the lid's jaw.

Gently probing the footlocker, he tried to identify what he felt: a hat, a shirt with a zillion buttons, papers rolled in tubes or folded, a round-cornered velvet-covered box. Slowly, he reached down—he wouldn't have reached down a booby-trapped tunnel more carefully—moving toward the side of the footlocker where he had seen the Purple Heart strike when his father threw it in. The thin skin covering his knuckles brushed against the side, and he spread his fingers wide.

His little finger bumped something hard, right where the side met the bottom. With that touch he knew he'd found what he'd been looking for.

Flipping the medal into his palm, he rubbed the pad of his thumb over it and felt its face.

Luke was amazed at the details he could feel with his thumb, how his thumb made the Purple Heart come alive. Perhaps it was being in complete darkness. Perhaps it was being able to see it in his mind's eye as it lay on the floor spotlighted by the flashlight.

The texture was almost the same as that of a quarter but fancier somehow—and more definite. He pictured what he felt: a profile of George Washington—different from a quarter because the high collar of an old-fashioned military uniform stuck up where his neck should be and because it wasn't round, but shaped more like a first grader's drawing of a heart. He knew that it was gold, not silver, with a heart-shaped layer of icy purple frozen on top of that. George Washington's profile in gold was melted partway into the purple.

The edges of this thing weren't squared off and corrugated, as a quarter's would be, but tapered like the dull edge of a letter opener. And it had a ribbon—he remembered it was purple with a white edge.

His fingers began to tremble. His father had gotten this medal for being wounded. In the dark of the closet, his mind churned out scene after scene of how that might have happened. He imagined his father skulking through thick un-

28

derbrush, silent as a jaguar. He imagined men trailing behind his father, eyes big and trusting, knowing that where his father went, they would be safe. And then the scene exploded into chaos—bombs went off and his mind suddenly filled with smoke that didn't allow him to see his father get wounded.

Part of Luke was glad—he didn't want to see his father get hurt. Even so, another part of Luke was disappointed. His father must have handled it bravely—gritted his teeth and shouted instructions for his own medical care to the horrified medic.

His hand tightened over the medal and his heart raced as he heard steps approaching, coming down the hall from his parents' bedroom. He held his breath and his ears lifted with straining to hear as the footsteps came up to the closet. His father? Come to rummage around in the footlocker again?

No. The footsteps were lumbering and heavy and he could picture his mother's widened gait, her feet flared outward more than usual. He began breathing again as she walked by and then into the bathroom. She didn't bother to close the door and he clearly heard the *clunk* as she lowered the seat onto the toilet bowl.

He wished that she'd closed the door as he tried not to listen to the other sounds and, finally, to the flush and sucking swirl of water. She walked past the closet again, and within moments the house was quiet again.

Slowly, carefully, quietly, Luke held the medal

in his left hand as he maneuvered the pinched boot from the jaw of the footlocker. Easing the lid down, he turned and opened the door.

Slinking down the hall, Luke held the Purple Heart tightly in one hand and cupped the other over his crotch. Fear pulsed through his body, and he imagined himself as an escaped prisoner-of-war, stripped naked as he snuck through the jungle, protecting that part of him that he imagined would be shot at before anything else.

He closed his bedroom door and crawled onto his bed, sliding his hand with the medal under his pillow as he laid his head down, his ear resting on his fist. The lump of his fist was uncomfortable, but he lay that way as if listening—listening for whatever the Purple Heart might tell him.

Luke heard nothing but blood pounding in his ears. And just as this drumbeat was about to lull him to sleep, the siren up the block began wailing, ordering people to seek shelter from an approaching storm.

Leaping from bed, Luke fumbled for his pajamas, which were in a pile by his bed, the top indistinguishable from the bottoms. He struggled to discover which was which.

His bedroom door opened and his mother's head popped in.

"You can put those on downstairs, honey. Come on, now, let's go."

"I'm coming," he said through his teeth, still struggling. "I'll be there in a minute." He heard his father's footsteps approach. The door swung open.

His father shone the flashlight at him, the beam hitting Luke right where he didn't want to be hit. "Hey!" he cried out, blocking the light with a wad of pajamas.

Before Vietnam his father might have smiled and cried: "It's a boy!" Now there wasn't a trace of humor in his eyes.

"Tornados don't care what you're wearing," his father said in a grim voice. His face looked as if he hadn't slept for several days. "You're better off buck naked and alive than dead and wearing your Sunday best. Get a move on!" he barked.

Wide-eyed, Luke did as his father said. He got a move on. Naked, he stumbled down the stairs in front of his parents, only then realizing that in his haste he'd left the Purple Heart under his pillow.

The storm hit moments later, just as Luke finished pulling on his pajamas, and just before he wriggled into his sleeping bag. The house shook, and Luke imagined it being pulled up as if it were a rotten tooth, basement and all.

He turned toward the wall, partly to avoid the light of his father's trembling flashlight and partly to avoid looking at him sitting with his back against the wall, staring straight ahead as if he were seeing ghosts. It gave Luke the creeps. He hadn't realized until now how thin and gaunt his father was, how drawn and sickly. He looked like the pictures of prisoners-of-war in *Life* magazine—men with raccoon eyes and cheekbones that were as sharp as their chins.

And now they were all—his mother, his father, himself—prisoners in this basement.

Luke silently cursed himself for his stupidity and hoped that the Purple Heart would be safe under his pillow upstairs, that it would still be there in the morning . . . along with the rest of the house.

CHAPTER

4

"Get a move on, Private!" Mike called over his shoulder to Luke. "They're gaining on us!" This afternoon it was Mike's turn to be sergeant.

As Mike darted down the sidewalk, zigging right and zagging left, he made a whistling noise and the ragged sound of a messy explosion. Luke, running behind, wouldn't have been surprised to see the sound rip through Mike's head, lifting its hairy top like a shag of grass blown skyward by a land mine.

"And watch for booby traps!" Mike barked, holding his arms crooked at the elbows, as if he were cradling a rifle or a machine gun. From half a block away, Mike looked as if he didn't have a neck, as if his head were rolling from rim to rim in the valley between his shoulders.

Luke ran as fast as he could, which wasn't as fast as Mike but fast enough, considering. For one thing he'd been awake most of the night, afraid to fall asleep because of the storm.

For another thing his right hand was jammed into the front pocket of his jeans, holding the Purple Heart. He wanted to be sure the medal didn't slowly work its way out of his pocket and then get dented or chipped by falling onto the sidewalk. Luke punched the air with his other fist, trying to catch up to Mike, without much luck.

Mike disappeared around the corner at the end of the block and was hidden by a tall, thick, shaggy hedge that grew over half the sidewalk. A few branches stuck out like threatening arms, poised to grab whatever ran by, as if warning passersby to steer clear of Mrs. Pederson's yard. Everybody steered clear of Mrs. Pederson regardless. Kids in the neighborhood grew up believing she was a witch.

Having a hand stuffed into his pocket made Luke's right shoulder curl forward and caused him to twist and lurch as he ran. His left leg reached out longer than his right leg, jarring him with each step. Luke ran as if he were wounded.

Wounded. *They got me!* he groaned to himself, the voice in his head deep and breathless, a voice he hoped sounded like his father's. "Dirty commies!" he coughed. Scrunching his face, he hoped it was like his father's during the heat of a pitched battle—creased and puckered around his eyes and mouth. Instead, without warning, he remembered his father's face at the airport, tears slicking down.

"Crud!" he muttered, shaking his head to rid it of what he was picturing.

He saw the chunk of broken cement on the sidewalk just before he stepped on it, but it was too late—he rolled over onto his right ankle, almost falling. Pain shot up his leg, growing enormous. Tears sprang to his eyes, almost spilling.

"Mike! Hey, Mike!" he cried out, his voice cracking, hoping that Mike hadn't already gotten so far ahead that he couldn't hear. "Wait up!"

Mike's head popped out from the hedge's corner. "What's keeping you, soldier?" he bellowed, sounding as much like a drill sergeant as he possibly could.

"I twisted my ankle . . . bad." Luke groaned in spite of himself. Mike narrowed his eyes and watched as Luke took several halting steps. He crossed his arms over his chest. "It's because you were running with your stupid hand in your stupid pocket. You've had your hand in there the whole ding-dang day and *now*"—Mike took a step toward Luke—"you'd better tell me what it is this time or . . ."

Great, thought Luke. Mike had been pestering him all day about what he had in his pocket and he'd refused to tell. And now that he was hurt, Mike was going to try to bully it out of him.

Let him try, Luke thought. He had his reasons for not telling. He knew how excited Mike would be to see and hold his father's medal. But he also knew that Mike would ask about how his father was wounded. Luke was embarrassed that he still didn't know any details.

"I told you already," Luke said. "I don't have *anything* in my pocket . . . except my hand." He jammed his hand deeper into the pocket and his shoulder slumped, causing his head to tip.

35

"You do so," Mike said. "And if you don't show me what it is, I'll *make* you show me."

Luke spoke slowly, measuring each word. "I don't have anything . . . that you should see."

"Oh yeah?" Mike's voice grew hard as he became Sergeant Trainer once more. "Atten-hut!" he shouted, squaring his shoulders and snapping his feet together.

If there had been any doubt in Luke's mind, Mike's attitude vaporized it. He didn't care how much Mike wanted to see the Purple Heart, he'd *never* see it if Luke could help it. Luke knew by the look on Mike's "Sergeant Trainer" face that Mike was determined and that he could not be trusted. But for right now, Luke decided it would be wisest to play along—to play for time.

He drew himself up and obeyed Mike's command.

"Salute your commanding officer, Private Canvin," Mike ordered.

Luke almost smiled. Mike could be tricky.

"Yes, sir!" Luke said. Because his right hand was in its pocket, he saluted Mike with his left hand (almost hitting himself in the eye), at the same time knocking the heels of his sneakers together and making a loud click with the back of his tongue against the roof of his mouth. Renewed pain from moving his ankle burned up his leg. "Private Canvin reporting for duty, sir!" he said through clenched teeth.

Mike's face hardened. "That wasn't a proper salute, soldier! What arm do you salute with? Huh, Private? Huh?" He took a step closer and

36

Luke's legs tightened and, keeping his head in one place, he searched for a way to escape. Even if he pulled his hand out of his pocket, it would be difficult to move quickly with a sore ankle, but he had to try.

Before Luke could answer, Mike's face suddenly softened. He was about to pounce—Luke could feel it in his bones.

"Hey, look, Luke," Mike said, smiling in a way that wasn't friendly, his words wheedling. "I won't tell anybody what you have in your pocket. Come on. I promise . . . honest. Cross my heart and hope to die."

Luke noticed that Mike's head was facing him, but that his eyes were looking off to the side, toward the hedge. From experience, Luke now knew from which direction Mike would attack.

Luke yanked his hand from his pocket, but before he could take a step Mike was all over him, grabbing his shoulders and pushing down with all his weight.

"Ow!" Luke bellowed, feeling his ankle melt into a puddle of pain. His knees buckled. Before he hit the sidewalk, Mike was grappling, trying to pull his right arm around his back into a hammerlock.

Luke squirmed and twisted and suddenly found himself facing Mike, who held his right hand in both of his.

"Let me see what you got," Mike grunted, trying to jam Luke's hand into the vise of his knees so he could pry it open.

"No!" Luke strained. Just as Mike got his right

37

wrist between his legs, Luke realized that he'd been concentrating so much on the Purple Heart that he'd forgotten to use his left hand. He grabbed Mike's shirt collar and twisted.

Mike looked up at him in surprise and then in anger. He grunted and fell over onto his side, keeping Luke's hand between his knees, pulling Luke with him. Luke tipped over and Mike scrambled on top. Luke glared at Mike, who was sitting on his chest, his teeth bared in his effort to pry open his hand.

"No!" Luke screamed. He closed his eyes and strained to keep his hand closed, to make it as hard as a walnut.

And then, with a feeling like a nut cracking, his hand popped open and Mike scampered away. "Crud!" Luke spat, hating himself for not being able to win against Mike when it was so important.

He heard Mike's gasp. "Wow! Is this your dad's?"

Luke rubbed his hand and his forearm, sullen and angry, but oddly relieved that he no longer had to keep the Purple Heart a secret from his closest friend. Reluctantly, he looked up.

"It isn't President Johnson's. Yeah, it's my dad's."

Mike came over to him, holding his hand out, palm up. The medal lay backside up. The light was such that it appeared to be a tiny, cupped pool of liquid gold. Mike held it out to him, and Luke gazed at the words etched onto the back:

FOR MILITARY MERIT. And right below that: Patrick Canvin.

"A Purple Heart," Mike whispered, awestruck. Luke took the medal by its ribbon from Mike's hand. "So," Mike continued whispering, "he got wounded, huh?"

Luke nodded, dreading the question he knew was coming next.

"How?"

Luke thought for a moment. "A bullet in the shoulder."

"Did he kill the guy that got him?"

Luke nodded and then sighed. "Yeah." He saw the hungry, curious look on Mike's face. "He shot him at close range and then popped off a bunch of other guys too . . . while he was waiting for the medic."

Mike nodded, turning shy, inspecting his own hand, which he'd scraped on the sidewalk from wrestling with Luke. And then he looked up, grinning. "Look. I'm wounded. Why don't you let me hold on to the Purple Heart for a while. I earned it."

Luke could feel anger buzzing around in his brain. He looked away from Mike, toward the hedge. "Sure," he said, "after I throw you into Mrs. Pederson's yard so she can make fertilizer out of you." His voice was tight.

He'd meant to sound awful. He'd meant to sound mean. But when he heard Mike's laugh, he realized how silly his threat had sounded. He looked at Mike, feeling more irritated than angry.

"Remember all those stories about Mrs. Pederson? You know, the ones Jake and his friends used to tell us?" Mike asked.

A tight smile slowly, almost painfully, grew on Luke's pinched face. He felt the texture of the Purple Heart with the pad of his thumb. "Yeah."

"Remember the one when she would rush out of her house with a butcher knife if we stepped on even one blade of her grass?" Mike laughed again. "And he told us that she fertilized her lawn with pets that she ground up so fast that their pieces were still alive when they hit the grass."

It was now Luke's turn to laugh, grudgingly.

"And how about her snatching bodies from the cemetery after they'd rotted for exactly a year? And then she'd bury them in her flower gardens and it didn't matter what color her flowers were supposed to be, they were red when they blossomed?"

Mike reached for Luke's hand, and Luke let Mike help him to his feet. Taking a cautious step, Luke found that his ankle wasn't as sore as he expected. In fact, it felt almost normal. Together, they rounded the corner of the block and Luke stared down the stretch of sidewalk that had always terrified him as a first grader walking to and from school. He and Mike had often held hands and run down this sidewalk, stealing glances at the opening to Mrs. Pederson's front yard, careful not to step on even the grass that grew between the squares of cement.

Luke looked at Mike. "And remember when I asked Jake why the police or the FBI or the marines or *somebody* didn't get her for doing those things? Remember what he said?"

Luke was embarrassed to think of that now and wondered if Mike felt the same way. "Yeah. The bell."

Mike whispered now, just as Jake had whispered when he'd told them this story. "Yeah. He said that she would ring her bell to call the ghosts of people who are still alive and that those ghosts would leave their bodies and *come* to her."

Luke stopped walking. "And he said that she hypnotized those ghosts and made the people they came from do anything she wanted."

Mike turned to Luke, covering his mouth with his hand to hold laughter in.

Luke's eyes narrowed. "I wonder," he said under his breath, "what would happen if *I* rang that bell. . . ."

Mike took his hand from his smiling mouth. "Cool." And then he frowned. "But *I* should be the one because *I'm* the sergeant today," he said.

"But *I* should be the one because it was *my* idea," Luke argued. He hated it when Mike pulled rank on him.

"I know what we're going to do," Mike said. "Draw sticks. The person with the shortest stick gets the honor." He broke two twigs from the hedge and stripped off the leaves. Turning his back to Luke, he arranged them in his fist so they both stuck up evenly, turned to face Luke, and held them practically under his nose.

Squeezing the Purple Heart extra hard for luck, Luke plucked a twig from Mike's fist and held it up to the one that remained in Mike's hand. He smiled.

Mike frowned. "Two out of three. . . ."

"No way! You stand guard out here and I'll go . . . go call for some ghosts."

Luke's ankle ached as he started toward the gap in the hedge leading to Mrs. Pederson's yard. But the pain lessened with each step and finally disappeared.

He veered left and slipped through the narrow opening.

CHAPTER

5

Light, sound—even air—seemed to disappear inside Mrs. Pederson's yard. Looking quickly to his left, Luke saw yellow, blue, purple, and orange flowers mixed with a sprinkling of red. He thought of how silly that story about the red flowers was.

The bell was supposed to be somewhere near the front porch, so he ran past two old, gnarled apple trees, one on either side of the sidewalk. The house appeared, seeming to cringe. Its front porch gaped, and the windows on either side were two glazed eyes. An image of Mrs. Pederson with a butcher knife cut through his thoughts.

To his left he spied an old bell hanging from a rusty metal arch that was mounted atop a wooden post stuck crookedly into the ground. A length of frazzled rope dangled from the side. Luke took two steps over the grass, slipped the Purple Heart into his pocket, and grabbed the rope.

Blood pumped in his ears as he yanked on the rope, which stretched slightly but didn't move. Tightening his grip on it, he drew himself up and threw his whole weight downward . . . leaning, grunting.

The rope groaned and Luke eased up, fearing that it would snap in two. Just then the bell broke free of its rust and clanged—tinny and rough—without an ounce of authority in its sound. Luke found himself looking up into the mouth of the bell, the clapper sitting in the darkness like a shriveled tongue.

He would have rung it again, but the bell froze where it was. It remained sideways, but the sound of its single, weak clang echoed in his head and set his teeth on edge.

Mission accomplished! he announced to himself, conjuring up his father's voice.

Letting go of the rope, Luke spun around and leaped toward the sidewalk. He began to run and then skidded to a halt.

It was as if she'd appeared out of thin air or had risen from the ground. She stood in the grass next to the sidewalk, facing him. He'd seen her from a distance many times before, but never this close. Her skin was stretched long with wrinkles and was so much like tissue paper that Luke would not have been surprised to be able to see through her to the flowers and hedge beyond. And her hair was a fuzzy white frost. Her feet were rooted in the grass and she leaned to his right, toward the sidewalk, crooked almost to the point of falling over, blocking his way. The only things about her that seemed alive were her dark eyes, which twitched in their sockets.

He shivered, knowing that she'd probably seen

44

him struggle with her bell, knowing that while he'd struggled she'd been able to position herself so as to block his way out of the yard.

And then he saw that she held a knife, its blade thin and delicate from too much sharpening. And in her other hand she clutched flowers of various sizes and shapes—all of them red.

A black hole erupted across her face. Her mouth! He panicked, feeling surrounded, trapped, *haunted.* All of those childhood fears that he'd thought were gone came alive, groping and sliding through his slimy innards. His heart ticked like a bomb set to explode at any moment, and before he could stop himself, he bellowed and ran across the yard, away from this apparition who was Mrs. Pederson. He didn't even slow down as he approached the towering wall of green but instead turned his shoulder to the hedge and rammed into it. Tucking his chin so as to protect his face, he fought through branches that grabbed and poked at him. The hedge seemed to lift him up—his feet no longer touched the ground.

Luke thrashed and kicked, grunting as he forced his way through the hedge. In his fury he thought he heard Mrs. Pederson yell with a voice that crackled—or was it the twigs and branches snapping off so close to his ears? It sounded like the word "Stop!" but he couldn't be sure, and even if it had been, he wouldn't have stopped for anybody or anything.

Suddenly Luke was through the hedge and on

the sidewalk, running harder than he'd ever run before.

From behind he heard Mike call his name, but he kept on running, feeling as if his heart were bursting and his lungs were shredding.

Luke squinted as he ran. Visions of Mrs. Pederson flashed in his mind like a nightmare slide show: *(click)* Mrs. Pederson leaning over the sidewalk, blocking his way—*(click)* Mrs. Pederson's face opening up into a black hole—*(click)* Mrs. Pederson's knife and the red flowers in her other hand—*(click)* the bell's mouth open as if to scream, its clapper a mummified tongue, but no sound coming out.

Luke opened his eyes wide to let daylight blind him to these images, and he ran until his fear was almost spent, until he could run no farther.

"Crud!" he muttered. He couldn't believe he'd been so scared of her, that he'd actually screamed and then run. As he slowed to a walk, he heard Mike's heavy breathing grow louder even before he heard the sound of his approaching footsteps. *What had gotten into him?* Luke felt as if somebody else—or *something*—had controlled his body for a moment.

The bell? Mrs. Pederson? He shuddered.

"Hey, Luke!" Mike gasped, stumbling up next to Luke. "What happened? Did you . . . did you see . . . see Mrs. Pederson?" he asked, gulping air. "Did she try . . . try to get you?"

Gulping air also, Luke thought of the knife, its blade so sharp and slim, and nodded.

"Whoo-eee!" Mike shouted, pushing himself up-

46

right and throwing back his head. He was breathing easier now. "I heard the bell and . . . and then I heard a yell," he said. "Or a scream . . . like swearing or something! Geeze, she sounded like a cat getting run over. I almost went in . . . in after you but then you came out . . . out of the *hedge!*" His eyes were full of admiration. "You were running so fast, I couldn't keep up with you!"

Luke stared back at Mike. Mike didn't know that Mrs. Pederson wasn't the one who screamed, didn't know how scared he'd been, didn't know that he hadn't been brave—that he'd run for his life, that *he'd* screamed, for cripe's sake. Mike had a dopey expression on his face and was looking at him as if he were some kind of hero, was looking at him as if he expected to hear all about the brave thing he'd just done.

"You did it!" Mike laughed, slapping Luke on the shoulder. "You rang her ding-dang, ding-dong bell!"

"Yeah," Luke said uncertainly.

"All *right!*" Mike slapped him again, almost knocking him over. "What happened? Come on. I gotta know! I gotta!"

Luke groaned before he could stop himself. He didn't feel up to inventing a fantastic story for Mike. He'd already told Mike lies about his father and Vietnam, and it was getting hard to keep them all straight. His eyes soured with tears as he looked at Mike, angry that Mike was making him feel as if he had to lie—again.

"Nothing," he mumbled. "Nothing much." He

looked at Mike, expecting to see disappointment, expecting to have to tell Mike to bug off. Instead, he saw more intense admiration in Mike's face.

"Oh, come on," Mike said, encouragement in his voice. "You can tell me. It's not like you're *bragging* or something. . . ."

Bragging? Mike couldn't have gotten it more wrong if he'd tried.

"I just ran in and rang the bell and . . ." Luke began to explain, but Mike was too excited to let him finish.

"And she just happened to be waiting—right?— to get you and you rang her bell anyway—right?— and you escaped. You got out of her yard . . . *alive!*"

Luke shut his mouth. Mike didn't want to know what really happened. Anyway, he wouldn't believe Luke now even if he told the truth on a stack of Bibles.

As they approached his driveway, Mike stopped and turned to Luke. "Wanna come in and watch TV?"

Luke was tempted. And he felt uneasy about going home, about having to be so quiet and careful around his father. But right now, more than anything, he wanted to be alone. He wanted to get home, go to his room, and sort out his feelings. "Naw," he said. "I need to, you know . . . help my mom with stuff."

"Aw, come on," Mike wheedled. "Just for a little while. I bet I could sneak us a few potato chips."

"No," Luke said, stubbornness pushing his jaw out.

Mike studied him for a moment. He nodded and stood at attention. "Permission for leave granted, Private!" he said in his sergeant's voice. "Report for duty tomorrow at oh eight hundred." And then he gave Luke a smart salute, spun on his heel, and marched up his own driveway.

★

Luke walked into the kitchen as quietly as he could. He paused to listen and didn't hear anything. The house felt empty—empty of people but filled with uneasiness.

Still he heard nothing as he sneaked through the kitchen and then through the living room—no groans or snores or creaking of floors—no water running or thump-thump of iron on ironing board. He sniffed, trying to detect the faint tell-tale smells of perfume or after-shave or the moist scent of soap that has just been used. He smelled nothing and should have begun to relax. But he couldn't. Something didn't feel right.

Quietly, barely breathing, he eased shut his bedroom door. He felt like such a sissy, being scared in his own house, and he thought of the way he'd been in Mrs. Pederson's yard. His heart quickened and he felt a shadow of the panic that had caused him to scream and run.

His gut crumpled as he doubled over to sit on the edge of his bed, propping his head on his hands, elbows wedged behind his kneecaps. His ankle pulsed in a dull way, a faint echo of the ache in his heart. Why had he acted that way?

Why had he lost his head like that? She's just an old lady, he scolded himself. It's just an old, rusty bell.

His father would never have acted like that. His father would have stood his ground—would have been brave enough to stick around, to take his lumps from Mrs. Pederson. Luke thought of the knife she'd held. Now, sitting in his room, it seemed ridiculous to think of Mrs. Pederson trying to stab him. His father would have known that.

Luke's hand moved toward the pocket with the Purple Heart. It was time to put it back where it belonged. Besides, after what had happened in Mrs. Pederson's yard, he didn't deserve to have it. He drew his hand away from the pocket. He knew that if he touched it now, took comfort in its feel, he wouldn't take it back.

Luke stood and walked to his bedroom door. He listened again for sounds of his parents but still he heard nothing. The silence yawned larger as he opened the door and glided down the hallway. Pulling open the closet door, he dropped to his knees in front of the footlocker, leaned to the left, and slipped his right hand into the right pocket of his jeans. His fingers spread apart, filling out the pocket, smoothing the cloth inside.

His eyes widened and his body went rigid. His fingertips touched nothing but lint-crusted cloth.

The Purple Heart was gone!

CHAPTER

6

The Purple Heart!
Luke's fingers wriggled, desperate to feel what was no longer in his pocket. He felt for holes through which the medal might have slipped, but there were no holes, only the tail of knotted thread that held together the pointed bottom of the pocket.

Where could it be? He swore he'd put it in his pocket before he rang the bell. His thoughts tripped over each other, stumbling backward, reeling, trying to remember when he'd last felt it, trying to think of where it might have fallen out.

The sidewalk? As he ran from Mrs. Pederson's yard? Maybe.

But he wasn't convinced, didn't *want* to be convinced. If it had fallen out on the sidewalk, somebody might have picked it up by now. Squeezing his eyes tighter, he tried to think of less horrible possibilities.

The hedge as he wrestled with the branches? He pictured a branch snatching the medal from where it had eased up from his pocket.

And then he thought of Mrs. Pederson's yard.

Groaning, he remembered putting the medal back into his pocket before he rang the bell. But he hadn't checked to make sure it was safe inside.

In his mind, Luke saw in slow motion what must have happened. He saw the Purple Heart dangle from his fingers as his hand moved toward his pocket. He saw his fingers release the medal and he saw the medal slide, skidding down the outside of his jeans, falling, sinking, disappearing into the grass.

Luke's head jerked sideways at the sound of a car door slamming shut next to the house. Scrambling to his feet, he closed the closet door just as he heard the creak of the kitchen door opening and his mother's voice call, "Yoo-hoo! Luke? We're home!"

He turned, his heart tripping over itself, just as his mother appeared in the hallway, a smile connecting her ears.

"Oh, I'm so glad you're here!" she said, coming up to him and taking him in her arms. "I was afraid that maybe you were at Mike's, watching television or . . . or whatever!" Holding his face in her hands, she took a step from him and patted one of his cheeks. "If I'd had to wait to tell you the news, I would have just . . . just gone crazy!"

"Hey." Luke looked over his mother's shoulder and saw his father, bent slightly at the waist, half in and half out of the shadow that cut slant-

52

wise across the hallway from the kitchen. "Howdy."

Luke's mother stepped aside, and Luke didn't know if he dared believe what he was seeing. His father stood with a smile on his face that almost matched his mother's. Even in the half-and-half light Luke saw a twinkle in his eyes, which made his sunken cheeks seem less grim.

"Come on in and let's have us a party." His father tipped his head toward the kitchen. "Come on! We've got somethin' to celebrate!"

Luke's mother took his arm in both of hers and whispered in his ear, "It's great to see him happy!" Luke swallowed and nodded.

This is what he'd been dreaming of since his mother had told him that his father was coming home. But what would happen to his father's happiness when he found out that the Purple Heart was gone? Luke cringed, knowing that his father's happiness would be blown to smithereens. And it would be Luke's fault. All Luke's fault.

His father was sitting in his usual chair at the table holding a beer can as Luke and his mother walked into the room's brightness. Helping his mother into her chair, Luke then sat in his own chair, not knowing what else to do. His father took a swig from the can in his hand, sucking instead of sipping, swallowing noisily, and then smiled at him.

"I'm signed up," his father began, "only this time it ain't the army. It's college! Can you believe it? Your old man's going to college." Luke jumped as his father slapped the table with his open hand. Luke's father laughed, but his laughter was uneasy. "Gonna be a college student! Maybe I should just grow out my hair and not wash it and maybe wear me a few beads and let a little mold grow on my face and call it a beard. Maybe I should get me some exercise marching in demonstrations and . . ."

"Your dad can't work as a bricklayer anymore," his mother interrupted, "because of his . . . because of his injury. So we decided to take advantage of the GI Bill and see what there was for him to study at the community college."

"Yeah," his father said, sucking again at his beer. "What do you think of your old man being in television?" His father looked and sounded less grim as he tipped another slug of beer into his mouth.

Luke's eyes widened. "Television?"

His father threw back his head and his Adam's apple bobbed as if he were drinking his own laughter. "You are the limit, Luke. I won't be *on* TV, you silly. I'll *fix* 'em. What with color television taking over, why we'll *never* have enough people to fix the danged things." His smile relaxed as he sat back in his chair. "Your mom and I went through the 'Help Wanted' section of the paper this morning, and the jobs that caught my eye were for auto mechanics and for TV repairmen. And the closest I want to get to grease is your mother's fried chicken." He winked at Luke's mother and then looked back at Luke. "Well, what do you think?"

54

"I . . . it's great." Luke forced up the corners of his mouth, even though, inside, he felt more like the sunken middle part of a smile. Making televisions work seemed more like magic than anything else. But the missing Purple Heart took all the joy from his father's news. Luke had to find it before his father discovered it was gone. He had to find it before all this happiness was destroyed. "Well," he said, trying to sound cheerful, "I've got some homework to do."

"Good for you!" His father leaned back in his chair, winced, and quickly sat up as he rekindled his smile. "We'll both have to do homework from now on. Maybe you can help me with mine . . . especially the math."

Luke forced himself to grin, thinking of those times when his father had tried to help him with his math. It always ended with his father stomping off.

As he turned to leave, his mother reached out and stopped him. "You're a good kid, Luke. You know that?" She smiled.

His mother's words should have made Luke feel wonderful. But he felt now like a total fraud. If she only knew, he thought: knew that he'd stolen his father's medal—and lost it.

Feeling betrayed by the world, he sat on his bed and tried to think of what he should do. He knew that he should search for the medal—the sooner the better. He realized he'd boxed himself into a corner by telling his parents he had homework. But he couldn't wait.

Closing his bedroom door, he walked past his bed, lifted the window, unhooked the screen, and then lowered himself feetfirst to the ground.

Scampering around the house and down the sidewalk, he slowed to a half walk, half run and tried to calm himself. He had to keep his wits about him. *What would Dad do?* As he went, he tried to take his mind off his growing fear by pretending he was his father, out on patrol in Vietnam.

There was danger at every turn. His heart pounded and he imagined himself carrying a rifle—an M-16. He was alone in the jungle, separated from the rest of his patrol and surrounded by the enemy. He walked with his knees bent and his shoulders hunched. His eyes shifted back and forth, looking for unblinking eyes in every bush and for heads to appear and disappear from the sides of every tree.

His ears tingled. The sound of cars became the distant droning of airplanes on bombing missions. The faint sound of a power mower became that of a helicopter, evacuating wounded soldiers from a battlefield. Luke reminded himself that these were friendly sounds—the enemy didn't have airplanes or helicopters.

It was the occasional silence that made the hair on the back of his neck prickly. The enemy was extremely silent. He began to sweat. The Vietcong could be anywhere. They *were* everywhere. Suddenly the danger seemed real. Pretending was no longer fun.

He imagined mines and booby traps—things called Toe Poppers and Bouncing Betties. He stepped carefully. The cracks between the blocks of sidewalk were trip wires, and exhaust pipes from parked cars were gun barrels, aimed to shoot him when he snagged his foot on a wire. Painted crosswalks, faint and delicate where cars ran over them, were swinging rope bridges stretched between rice paddy irrigation ditches, bridges that were built to break in two at the thin parts.

Nothing could be trusted.

And then, before he felt ready, he rounded a corner and Mrs. Pederson's hedge stretched away from him. Vietnam disappeared and he was suddenly back in Iowa. His eyes roved up and down the scraggly row of bushes, searching for the place from which he'd emerged onto the sidewalk. He walked toward a likely spot, marked with a broken branch that stuck out over the sidewalk, its leaves wilted. Grabbing this branch, he elbowed his way into the thicket.

He strained to be silent, but twigs snapped and leaves rustled. He bowed his head to protect his face and also to search the gaps between the stalks for the medal. Just in case.

Before he stepped from the protection of the hedge, Luke scoped out the yard and tiny house. The ridge of the house sagged in the middle, and the white paint on its sides was flaking off, showing dark wood underneath, reminding Luke of peeling gray patches of dead skin. Shadowy white lace curtains fringed the tops and sides of the windows—the kind of curtains that you can look through from the inside without being seen from the outside.

And there were more old apple trees in the yard than he remembered—old and gnarled and covered with patches of small leaves that didn't look healthy. Even though apple blossoms had come and gone, Luke saw no apples.

Tensing, he heard the drone of voices to his left. He turned his head and saw several heavy bumblebees dive-bombing Mrs. Pederson's flowers. He relaxed—the bees were making the voice sounds.

He crouched to prepare himself and sucked in the kind of deep breath he took before jumping into a swimming pool. He eased himself out of the hedge and slowly crawled on his elbows to the nearest apple tree. He tried to pretend he was in Vietnam, on patrol, trying to locate an enemy camp. For once, his imagination failed him.

Peering around the trunk, he studied the house. He felt he was being watched—from where, he couldn't tell. He snaked around the tree and across the lawn, dragging his legs to keep his butt low, and glanced up at the house every few seconds as he searched the grass with his eyes and the flat of his hands.

From a distance the lawn looked smooth. But as Luke searched, he saw that it was sparse and cut too short. The dirt between the blades of grass felt lumpy and uneven, with shiny piles of the thin, stringy dirt that comes from burrowing worms.

As he approached the base of the bell post, the feeling that he was being watched grew stronger. Luke looked up to the house, and the corner of his eye caught a motion that looked as if a side curtain had just fallen back into place. He lunged toward the spot where he'd stood to ring the bell and frantically searched the area, scampering empty-handed to the safety of the nearest apple tree. His heart beat and his breath came in little wheezing gasps.

Had she seen him? Luke waited . . . and listened. *Was it a cat playing with the curtain? Or were his eyes tricking him?*

Luke waited, willing his breath to be normal. With each breath he thought about the only other place the Purple Heart might be. Mrs. Pederson could have found it and taken it inside. And if she had it inside, he would have to ask her for it—go up to her door and knock and ask her for it. He would have to do this thing like a soldier. That's what his dad would have done.

Luke got up, brushed off the knees of his jeans, and stood at attention. As he marched to the porch, he tried not to look at the bell, but he noticed that it still lay sideways, its mouth open in a silent scream. Snapping his eyes forward, he clomped up the porch stairs to the warped screen door.

He reached out and rapped, so hard that his

knuckles smarted. Still standing at attention, Luke kept his eyes forward and his shoulders square. He listened for footsteps, heard only silence, and rapped again.

CHAPTER

7

Luke stood in front of the door, feeling taunted by the silence.

"Mrs. Pederson!" he cried, and banged on the door with the flat of his hand.

He could hear faint noises outside the hedge—cars mostly, and birds. But the house seemed to exist in a bubble that somehow mixed sound with light so that they became the same sensation—a sensation he felt with his whole body, not just his ears and eyes. He was certain that Mrs. Pederson heard him knock as she held the Purple Heart in her hands, gloating as she stroked George Washington's cheek with her fingers.

He kicked the door and screamed, "Hey! I know you're in there." Again he waited. Still, nothing happened and Luke let an enormous grunt of frustration explode from his gut.

He reached out and tried the doorknob with a jerk of his wrist. It didn't budge. "Come on!" he half cried and half moaned.

He kept his hand on the knob, leaned forward, and rested the top of his head on the door. Maybe she's deaf and has turned off her hearing aid, he

61

thought. Maybe she's napping. Or maybe she's hurt inside and can't come to the door.

And then the worst possibility of all occurred to him: Maybe Mrs. Pederson had somehow died since he'd seen her and was in a heap on the floor, the Purple Heart imprisoned in her hand.

He snapped upright and let go of the knob. Hunched over and careful, Luke peered into the windows on either side of the door. The house was dark inside, and the glass of each window seemed coated with an oily layer of grime. He crept around the house but the darkness and the grime made it impossible to see inside.

He tested each window and found them all either locked, painted, or swollen shut. As he made his way around the house, the fear within him grew. Something had happened to Mrs. Pederson. If she was hurt or dead, the Purple Heart might be lost and never returned.

Trying the last window, he decided that he should call Mrs. Pederson on the telephone and if she didn't answer that he should call the police and tell them to check on her. He wouldn't have to give them his name. And if they asked how he knew something was wrong, he would tell them that he could smell something dead from outside her house.

Luke didn't dare leave Mrs. Pederson's yard by the front walk—he didn't want anybody to see him leave and think that he'd had anything to do with her being hurt or dead. He went to a far corner to push his way through the hedge and ran home.

★

Just as he opened the kitchen door, he remembered that he'd left the house from his bedroom window and that he should have come into the house that way. But it was too late. Three pairs of eyes turned to look at him as he stood in the doorway. And one pair was the dark, twitching eyes of Mrs. Pederson herself.

How did she know where to come? Maybe she *is* a witch, Luke thought.

His mother's eyes grew large and she began to get up from her chair.

His father reached out a hand from where he sat, gesturing her to stay where she was. "I told you he'd be back . . . in his own sweet time." His father was smiling but in his eyes Luke saw the stranger he'd bumped into in the hallway on the night his father came home. And, just as he had that night, Luke dropped his gaze from his father's face. It was then he saw the Purple Heart, looking small and fragile in the middle of the table.

Luke leaned into the doorframe for balance. He looked up as his mother spoke. "We were just talking about you," she said. "Mrs. Pederson said that you . . . that this afternoon you . . . that you ran into her yard and rang the bell she has by her front porch."

Fearfully, Luke looked from his mother's carefully polite face to his father's. He found no comfort there. His father's face was struggling to keep from looking angry, but anger bubbled up

63

in his face—in his eyes, in his mouth, in a tic in his cheek—bubbled up and disappeared and bubbled up again, like the surface of slowly boiling water.

He felt cast out by his parents. As if commanded, his eyes turned toward Mrs. Pederson. The old woman stared back at him, her shocking white eyebrows bristling.

"I had half a mind to keep it." Her voice didn't sound at all like the voice he'd heard this afternoon. It was old and thin, but it was also smooth. She glanced at the table, at the Purple Heart. "I knew what it was the moment I laid eyes on it. My Elijah had one from the Second World War."

Luke's father cleared his throat. "I believe you have some apologizing to do . . . to Mrs. Pederson here . . . for what you did this afternoon."

Luke felt a tightness in his throat that almost cut off his breath. "I'm sorry," he said, looking down at his feet.

"That's a poor excuse for an apology." His father seemed to sift his words through his teeth, letting the polite words out, keeping the hot, angry words inside his mouth where they appeared to be burning his tongue.

Luke's mother reached out and tried to soothe the back of his father's hand, which lay open next to the Purple Heart. "Luke," she said quietly, "you gave Mrs. Pederson quite a shock, and we've decided . . . the three of us have decided that . . ." She looked at Luke, closed her mouth, and tried to smile. Nodding toward the wall, next to Luke, she said, "Luke, grab that chair and sit down.

64

Tell us what you were doing in her yard . . . why you did that."

Luke didn't trust his body. Keeping a hand on the wall for support, he eased himself into the chair.

He forced his head up and faced Mrs. Pederson. In his head he heard a mocking voice: *Name, rank, serial number. Name, rank, serial number.* He cleared his throat to silence this voice. "I . . . Mike and I heard stories . . . and I just wanted to ring the bell!" he blurted out, the anger with himself mixed up with his words to Mrs. Pederson.

Mrs. Pederson's eyes flashed, mistaking his anger for defiance. "If you were my boy . . ." she said in a voice that rose with each word.

"I'm sure Luke will be happy to help you out . . . just as we agreed," Luke's mother said, quickly.

Mrs. Pederson ignored Luke's mother. "Don't think I don't know about the stories people tell. Don't think I don't know what people say." Her words were clear, even though her voice wavered.

Luke was startled by the crab quickness of her hands as she reached for the Purple Heart. The knuckles of her fingers were swollen, and each segment of each finger grew out at an odd angle. "If I hadn't found *this,*" she said, lifting it up from its ribbon, "I wouldn't have known whose parents to talk to. If you were my boy . . ." she repeated, dropping the medal to the table. Luke winced, fearful that the purple plastic would chip.

"We're glad you came to see us." Luke was sur-

65

prised to hear such calm words come from his father's stormy face. "We're truly sorry for the trouble Luke caused you, but we're grateful you let us know . . . so we could nip this thing in the bud."

Mrs. Pederson nodded and looked from Luke to Luke's father. "I should expect to see Luke tomorrow?"

"Yes," Luke's father said. "First thing, seeing as how it's Saturday. And every day after school next week too. And I'll come over sometime around noon to see to it that he's working hard enough."

Mrs. Pederson nodded. "Good."

"Luke, would you help Mrs. Pederson home . . . make sure she gets there okay?" His father was giving an order, barely disguised in politeness.

Luke nodded and leaned forward, preparing to stand.

"I can make my own way home." Mrs. Pederson stepped toward the kitchen door and paused before she pushed it open. "I will see you tomorrow, Luke Canvin, at eight o'clock," she said, looking at Luke. "And you can't call saying you're sick. I don't have a telephone."

★

Luke stared at the clasped hands in his lap, waiting for the silence to break, getting more tense the longer it lasted. It was as if he were in the kitchen alone—he couldn't even hear his

66

parents breathing. When he looked up, he felt shot down by the four eyes that stared at him.

His mother spoke first.

"We've always expected better of you . . ." she began, and then quickly closed her mouth, sucking in her bottom lip and frowning. "I mean . . . Luke, we . . . I just don't know *what* to think. When Mrs. Pederson came here and asked for you, I thought you were in your room doing homework and then . . . we saw you'd slipped out the window. And then Mrs. Pederson showed us your father's Purple Heart and we . . . I just couldn't *believe* it. And *then* she told us how she got it. Well . . ." Luke felt his chest tighten as he watched his mother struggle to remain calm. She was trying too hard to make it easier for them all. He wished that she would just yell, get it out, get it over with.

But his father's anger changed all that.

He picked up the Purple Heart. "You stole this from me." He spoke in a hoarse near-whisper. "You stole it and then you shamed me." Luke's throat tightened as he watched his father shift his weight in his chair and wince.

"How could you!" he shouted, and both Luke and his mother jumped. "You"—and his father pointed a shaking finger at Luke, aimed right for Luke's throat—"you have shamed me and hurt me. . . ." Spittle exploded from his mouth with each word. "You have *wounded* me"—he banged on his chest—"and I don't know *what* to think anymore."

Luke braced himself, too shocked to cry out.

67

His father stumbled to his feet and walked to him.

"If you want to be a hero so much, *here!* Take it! *Take* it!" His father tossed the Purple Heart at Luke's chest. It bounced, stinging, and landed on top of his hands.

His father walked to the refrigerator, limping more now than Luke had seen before. He tore open the door and grabbed a beer and stormed into the living room.

Luke looked down at the medal in his lap. A sob rose from his core and he closed his eyes and strained to open his mouth wide enough to let it out. His jaw pushed against his swollen chest. And then he felt his mother's arms around him and her breath brushed his ear as she spoke.

"Luke, don't . . . don't . . . it's all right, Luke . . . we love you, Luke. Your father loves you." He felt the bulge of her belly press against him and wished he could crawl inside her. "You're a good boy, Luke. Your dad knows that . . . we know that."

Shaking his head, gasping for air, he felt tears falling on his hands.

CHAPTER

8

"I don't want to go," Luke said, under his breath but loud enough for his mother to hear as she worked at the stove, her back to him.

"I don't imagine you do," she said, her words clipped. She turned around, bringing him a plate of scrambled eggs and toast. "But I think it's only fair."

"All I did was run in to her yard and ring her stupid bell." He stared at the plate. Sometimes he thought of golden yolks as the brains spilled from head-shaped shells.

"Luke," his mother said as she sat across the table from him, "I know you don't want to go, but I hope you understand why you're going. What you did . . ." Her eyes were impatient, and she let out her breath with a sigh. "You really did it up in a big way . . . when you decided to stir things up . . . make a little excitement." She made her voice goofy, trying to transform what she said into a joke.

Luke wasn't fooled. He turned his head toward the window but continued looking at his mother from the corner of his eye. She was more tired

69

than usual. Luke knew that she'd had a bad night—he had too. After Mrs. Pederson left, his father had continued drinking can after can of beer, until he passed out on the living room couch. Luke had never seen his father this way before. Before Vietnam, it seemed to Luke that his father grew more lively and cheerful when he had a few beers. But last night his father had grown quieter. His eyes had seemed to retreat into his head, peering at the world like those of a wild animal from the shadows of a cave, peering from under the ledge of his brow at his mother and at him as if they were somehow dangerous. He growled his words, as if warning them to keep their distance but to stay where he could see them.

Finally, Luke and his mother had half carried, half helped his father to his parents' bedroom. He'd been surprised at how light his father was. Before Vietnam, Luke wouldn't have been able to help lift him any more than he could help his mother pick up a car.

When he'd helped his mother take off his father's shoes, he had seen a dark stain growing from the fly of his father's pants. Luke had watched in horror as his father made a huge puddle on the floor. His father must have peed for thirty seconds, maybe a minute, and not even known it. His mother had tried to laugh about it, saying she needed practice changing diapers, what with the baby coming. But her laughter came out as hiccuping sobs.

Luke had gone to bed with an anxious, fearful

buzzing in his head. He'd caused his father to act the way he had, and he was scared that his father would never be the same again. Once more, in the middle of the night, he was awakened by his father's bellowing, louder than ever.

★

His mother shifted her weight on the chair and looked out the kitchen window. "Your father had a rough night, Luke. I'm sorry you had to be there when . . ." She sat up straighter, trying to look strong but sounding wrung out. "But, you know, healing takes time. He's going to be all right."

"Sure," Luke muttered, picking up a fork and poking at his eggs without looking at them. She'd said that once before, the day she'd told him his father was coming home from a hospital in Tokyo. It hadn't been true then and it wasn't true now.

"What did you say, Luke?"

Startled, Luke looked up to his mother's blazing eyes. As he struggled to find words to take back what he'd said, the fire in her eyes died and she sighed. "I know you didn't mean to do anything hurtful," she said, sitting back in her chair and resting her hands on her stomach. "I . . . I know you weren't trying to hurt any of us on purpose, Luke. But . . ." She rubbed one of her eyes in the way of a tired little kid. "Do you see what I meant when I asked you to be careful . . . to be quiet?"

71

Luke nodded, feeling miserable—about what he'd done to his father, about what he'd done to his mother, about how his father was acting. This misery was heaped upon the misery he already felt about having to go to Mrs. Pederson's house.

"Oh, Luke," his mother said, leaning forward as if over a barrel, reaching across the table, almost sticking her elbow into the eggs. She cupped his chin in one hand, lifting his face so that his eyes looked directly into hers. "It's a raw deal for all of us. It just isn't fair . . . what your dad is going through, what we're going through. But that's life . . . it's just one of those things." She was now close to tears. "I'm sorry . . . sorry as I can be." She let go of his chin. "You'd better eat those before they get cold," she added.

"I'm not hungry," Luke mumbled, not wanting to disappoint her further by being ungrateful, but knowing that he'd throw up if he tried to eat the eggs. He pushed the plate to the middle of the table.

"Luke," his mother said, sighing, "I want you to have enough zip to get through the day. There's no telling what Mrs. Pederson will have you do."

She looked behind him and he sensed a change in the room. "Good morning, honey," his mother said. She sounded uncertain.

Without a word, Luke's father walked toward the table and was just about to sit when a knock came from the kitchen door. Pausing for a moment, as if confused, Luke's father continued across the kitchen and opened the door.

72

"Is Luke here?" Mike's voice filled the room. "Sir," he added, sounding somewhat shy. From where he sat, Luke couldn't see Mike but he could picture him looking up at his father, his eyes bigger than normal, his mouth hanging open like a puppy's.

"Yes," his father said in a rasp, and then cleared his throat.

"Can he come out and . . . and play?"

Luke's father cleared his throat again. "No," he said in a flat voice. "He's busy today."

"Oh." In the silence that followed, Luke sensed that Mike wanted to ask why. But if he did, he must have chickened out. "Okay. 'Bye," he said in a voice that faded, sounding as if Mike were already running down the driveway.

Luke's father closed the door and turned around. The puffy skin around his eyes was blackened, almost as if somebody had socked him in each eye. His hair was spiky with grease. Even his ears looked droopy—saggy and wrinkled and old. And his mouth didn't seem to know what to do with itself.

Easing himself down onto the chair next to Luke, he looked at him with red-rimmed, sleep-crusted eyes. "I must have been a barrel of laughs last night," he said, half whispering, squinting so that he could focus on Luke's face, which he was having trouble doing. "Crud! I haven't . . . haven't done that for . . . since . . . Saigon."

Luke's father blinked, long and hard, and

73

opened his eyes to look down at the plate of eggs. "Those yours?" he asked.

Luke shook his head.

His father took hold of the plate, pulled it over, and began shoveling the eggs into his mouth, his hand trembling, chunks of egg tumbling off the fork with each bite. Luke watched his father chew and was disgusted to see bits of scrambled eggs clinging to a corner of his mouth. Pushing his chair back, Luke mumbled, "I gotta go."

"I'll come check on you . . . later this morning," his father said through the food in his mouth, his face only inches from the plate.

Luke took another, longer route to Mrs. Pederson's house. As he walked, he tried to make believe he was on a military patrol, making his way through the jungles of Vietnam. He tried to feel the way he'd felt yesterday, feeling the jungle air and hearing the sounds of battle.

But he wasn't a soldier in Vietnam. He wasn't his father. He was Luke Canvin, a stupid, scrawny boy in the middle of Iowa. His mouth was clamped so tight that the backs of his jaws ached. In his ears he heard a high-pitched hum.

He tried to relax and caught himself just before he thrust his hands into the pockets of his jeans. Letting his arms flop to his sides, he felt the Purple Heart each time he took a step. Each time he lifted his leg, it wedged itself deeper into the narrowing-widening crook where the base of his hip met the top of his leg. He didn't want to touch the Purple Heart, to be reminded of the crisis he'd created by taking it. In fact, he didn't want to have it with him at all. But he'd been afraid to give it back to his father—afraid of how his father would react. And he'd been reluctant to leave it in his bedroom, where it would have nagged him all day. Instead, he'd pinned it to the inside of his pocket so that it wouldn't work its way out and get lost.

The walk to Mrs. Pederson's house was over sooner than Luke would have liked. As he approached the gap in her hedge, his steps became stiffer, more hesitant.

He tried to push his feelings of misery aside along with an unruly branch from the hedge, but they followed him even as the branch snapped back to position. Luke turned up the sidewalk and walked toward the porch, stumbling over the first step. Taking a deep breath, he heard the humming in his ears grow louder. Raising his right hand almost in a salute, he rapped and waited, heard nothing inside the house, and rapped again.

After a few moments the faint sound of footsteps approached from the other side of the door. He was seized by a desire to turn and run, but his legs were locked in place. And then, level with his stomach, the knob in front of him twisted and the door opened a crack. Luke couldn't see anything in the narrow opening and he didn't know what to do. After a few moments the door opened wider, and Luke found himself looking into Mrs. Pederson's face.

Luke stared, suddenly not feeling any part of himself from the neck down. It was as if his head were filled with helium and floating in air anchored by a thin string that he himself was stepping on.

"Come in, Luke Canvin," she said, sounding almost shy. And then she disappeared. He heard her footsteps as she walked away from him.

Luke felt his body materialize, twice as heavy as before. He eased the door open and slipped inside. The hall was empty. Its hollow dimness seemed to push the ceiling and walls upward and away, making the house appear much larger on the inside than it looked from the outside. The hallway's musty smell reminded him of the air released from his father's opened footlocker. Trying not to make a sound, he walked toward the dim light at the end of the hallway and stepped into the kitchen.

The kitchen was hidden in shadows that seemed to shift toward whatever he looked at. Everything in the kitchen was old: the refrigerator, the small table next to the window—everything looked like black-and-white photos in yellowed *Life* magazines. Even the light coming from the window seemed somehow aged.

The kitchen also smelled old, as if the odor of boiling potatoes had soaked into the walls and floor and ceiling and could never be scrubbed out.

But Mrs. Pederson looked older than anything in the kitchen. She stood by the little table in

76

front of the window. Luke was surprised to see a large scrap of cloth—a scarf or a dishtowel—wrapped around her head like a turban. Over her dress she was wearing an apron with large ruffles sewn onto the straps, giving her big shoulders. And she leaned her hand on the table next to a squat, bluish carnival glass vase filled with flowers. The light in the room was such that he couldn't exactly tell what color they were.

Red, perhaps?

"I have some things for you to do . . . some lifting and cleaning," she said. "And I have some boxes under my bed that I want carried up to the attic and some things from the attic brought down here." She was all business but, unlike yesterday, she no longer seemed angry. Instead, she seemed somewhat ill at ease about having him in her house. He followed her from the dim kitchen to an even dimmer bedroom.

Not waiting for instructions, he dropped to his hands and knees and burrowed his head and shoulders under her bed. There was lots of dust—as he moved, it rippled almost like waves on a lake. He took little, quick breaths to avoid breathing it in. Even so, dust stiffened the inside of his nose, smelling faintly of talcum powder.

"There should be two small boxes on your right." Mrs. Pederson sounded as if she were in the next room. "Bring those out . . . if you would."

Carrying the two boxes, he followed her through the kitchen to the other side of the house where, in the middle of the ceiling, a trapdoor was flopped open. An old ladder stuck up into the darkness. Mrs. Pederson stopped at the base of the ladder and turned to look at Luke. "You go up the ladder first, and I'll be right behind—to tell you where to put them. Don't want to be at the top of the ladder with you down there peeking at my knickers." And then she laughed, a high nervous laugh, surprising Luke with its pleasantness.

The attic—really only a crawl space, with no room to stand up— was packed with things that seemed to take up the space where there should have been air for breathing. As Luke crouched near the trapdoor, Mrs. Pederson's head popped up next to him. She looked around her, squinting. "Sometimes my brain feels stuffed with junk, just like this attic," she said, a tiny smile playing with the corners of her mouth. "Why don't you take that box over there," she continued, pointing now, "and move it over here." Luke crawled toward the box, easing the weight of each hand and knee onto the boards in case they were rotted or split.

It seemed that Mrs. Pederson had him move everything in the attic at least once to make enough room for the boxes he'd carried up. The dust was thicker in the attic than under Mrs. Pederson's bed, in layers so thick that it looked almost as if he could pick it up and shake it like a heavy wool blanket. He sneezed frequently, and each time Mrs. Pederson said, "Bless you, Luke Canvin." Sometimes she barely got out that blessing before he sneezed again, and she'd repeat herself without pausing for breath.

"That's enough for now," she finally said, her

tiny smile growing larger. "I'm afraid you'll blow the roof off with your next sneeze."

Luke looked at her, his eyebrows rising in surprise, and smiled. "I'm sneezing the floor clean . . . up here," he said, hesitantly, not knowing how Mrs. Pederson would take his little joke.

She laughed—a more confident laugh than he'd heard earlier. "That's enough for now," she repeated, and Luke didn't know for a moment if she meant joking or work. "Oh, one more thing," she said, squinting up at him. "That wooden box . . . the carved wooden box up there . . . the one about this big?" And she had her flattened hands apart a little more than a foot.

He peered around, spotted it close by, and nodded.

"Bring it down. And be careful of it, Luke Canvin," Mrs. Pederson called. "Be careful."

CHAPTER

9

Luke was careful, but even so he banged the edge of the box on several rungs of the ladder as he made his way down, fighting for balance with each step. The box was much heavier than he had expected it to be, and its varnished surfaces were slick in his dust-powdered hands. He dug his fingers into the crevices of the deep carvings that covered its sides and cringed each time the box hit a rung, expecting Mrs. Pederson to reprimand him. If she noticed, she didn't say a thing.

As he came down the stairs, Luke wrestled not only with the box but with his feelings about Mrs. Pederson. She was nothing like he thought she should be, and he felt tricked. She actually joked around, even poking fun at herself. It was this sense of humor that confused him the most.

The box seemed to grow heavier. His arms were more tired than he realized from shifting boxes in the attic, and they seemed to stretch longer with each step. By leaning backward he was able to keep from dropping what he held.

As he followed Mrs. Pederson to the kitchen, he wondered how the stories about her being a witch had gotten started. He couldn't imagine her being anybody's grandmother, but she didn't seem like witch material, either. She was bird-like—her head moved forward slightly with each step, reminding Luke of a pigeon walking.

Maybe, he thought, she had done something bloody and unspeakable in the past. Maybe she had an evil side that he hadn't seen yet. Or maybe she was nice until your guard was down and then ... *wham-oh!* Would she now turn around and grab a knife and run after him?

She turned around and Luke tensed, expecting the worst. Instead of seeing crazy eyes and anger, he saw a smiling face. It was not an easy smile— her face didn't seem used to smiling—but it was nice enough.

"You can put the box on the table, Luke Canvin," she said, never taking her eyes off him.

Walking to the table, he eased the box onto its Formica top, which appeared glassy in the kitchen's light, nicked and scratched in patterns that reminded him of the ice on a skating rink. As he sat, Luke saw that the carving on the box made a dense pattern of leaves and vines.

She sat across from him, and there was a stretch of uncomfortable silence as Luke stared at the box, wondering what was inside it.

Mrs. Pederson took a sharp, deep breath and looked at Luke. "I thought you'd be interested to see some things in this box." She nodded toward it. Pulling the box toward her, she lifted the lid. She reached in and bent so low over the open box that Luke wondered if she was trying to find something by its smell. Concentrating changed her face completely as thousands of tiny wrinkles appeared, making her ugly.

"My Elijah got several decorations in the war," she said in a soft voice that was hollow from speaking into the box. "He served his country well, Luke Canvin. He was a hero . . . to me." Her face suddenly relaxed, and most of the wrinkles disappeared. "Ah, here it is." She sighed. It was spooky, as if there were two Mrs. Pedersons in the same body—one more wrinkled than the other and each taking turns appearing on her face.

She sat up and pulled her hand from the box. "His Good Conduct Medal."

Luke stared, dumbstruck, as she laid it on the table and then began rooting around in the box again.

"How did he . . . what did he do to get it?" Luke asked, his hand inching toward the medal. He wanted to touch it but didn't know if he should.

"I don't know," she said, pausing in her rummaging to gaze at it.

The medal was gold colored and round. Circling it were the words EFFICIENCY, HONOR, FIDELITY. An eagle, wings spread, stood on a long sword laid across the cover of a closed book.

"He must have been a good soldier, though," she said, looking up at Luke.

Luke glanced at Mrs. Pederson and back down to the medal. It didn't look heroic—unlike his father's Purple Heart.

Mrs. Pederson plunged her hand into the box

82

again. "There," she said, smiling, drawing out another medal.

Luke sucked in his breath. This medal was beautiful, a robed woman standing with a crown of light rays. She had wings and held a sword in one hand, pointing down as if she were ordering somebody to kneel. In the other hand she held a shield. "What is it?" he asked.

"A Victory Medal," Mrs. Pederson said. "Practically everybody got one for serving in the war."

"Oh." Luke was disappointed to hear that.

Once more Mrs. Pederson bent over the box. "Ah, here's the one I thought you'd like to see." She pulled her hand from the box, and Luke instantly recognized its heart shape. She held it above the table and stared at it herself. It twisted slowly on its ribbon, going first one way and then the other, showing both sides. It was like his father's but older-seeming, softer. It was the difference between a shining new quarter and a quarter that had spent years in hundreds of pockets, rubbing and clinking against other coins. "Here," she said, reaching toward Luke. He held out his hand, and she dropped it into his palm, backside up.

There, etched below the motto FOR MILITARY MERIT was a name that sounded as if it came from the Bible: Elijah Pederson.

He looked from the medal to Mrs. Pederson and found she was looking at him, her chin almost resting on her chest, her eyes steady and calm. He wanted to ask her how her husband had been wounded. He wanted to know the story.

83

He wanted to know because it seemed that knowing the story of Elijah Pederson would bring him closer to knowing what had happened to his father.

It was as if she'd read his thoughts. "Elijah never told me much about the War. I learned more from the newspaper and the newsreels than I ever learned from him. All I know is that it must have been terrible . . . the bombing, the marching, the rain, the mud, the barbed wire . . . the stink of death." She pulled her shoulders back and her face tightened, becoming more stern. "He was a quiet man, my Elijah . . . a peaceful, quiet man. He kept his thoughts to himself . . . and his feelings. And I never pried. I never pestered him the way some women do."

Luke nodded and swallowed his disappointment.

Mrs. Pederson nodded along with him. "I wondered too, Luke Canvin. Often, as I watched Elijah go into the orchard in the morning, a little hitch in his step, I wondered what dreadful things he carried in his heart. I only know that he did what he had to do . . . he did his duty and he defended his country by risking his life. I only know that he didn't enjoy it . . . it brought him no joy, the killing. But he must have done it, and it must have made him hurt fearsomely each time he killed another man."

She looked down at the wooden box. "I loved him for his quietness. But I do wish that he'd unburdened himself . . . a little. He might have lived longer. . . ." She looked up, and Luke saw a glistening in her eyes and embarrassment hardening her mouth.

"Well, I suppose we'd better get back to work," she said briskly. "I would like you to do some cleaning"—she smiled, as if she were telling a joke on herself—"dusting under things . . . where I can no longer reach."

Luke held out the Purple Heart, and just as she took it, they both froze, their arms stretched across the table, their fingers almost touching. The feeble sound of a bell drifted through the kitchen. It was followed by the rush of a clearer, brighter ring. And then another and another.

Mrs. Pederson gasped, and her hand thumped to the table. Horrified, Luke looked into Mrs. Pederson's face. As if in a remembered nightmare, he saw a hole open, swallowing her face. Her mouth! Her throat had tightened, but instead of a scream, a terrifying silence poured from her mouth followed by a wheezing rattle that formed the words "Stop them! Stop them!"

Luke leaped from his seat and ran through the hallway to the front door. While he ran, the ringing stopped. Gasping now, he threw open the door and grabbed the jamb to stop himself from tumbling outside. He stared, not believing what he saw.

Mike ran down the sidewalk, his shoulders hunched, his head swaying back and forth.

And just as he neared the end of Mrs. Pederson's sidewalk, Luke watched his father's frame step into the gap in the hedge, filling it right where Mike was aimed.

85

Suddenly Mike saw Luke's father. He pulled himself up, trying to keep from ramming the man's stomach. Luke's father's arms shot upward to fend off the body hurtling toward him.

Luke closed his eyes against their falling—but not seeing was worse than seeing. Opening his eyes, he saw his father falling, Mike sprawled on top of him. The moment his father hit the pavement, he scrambled to his feet, grabbing Mike's shirt collar, pulling him off the sidewalk with a strength that didn't match his shrunken body. His father held Mike by the nape of his neck, and Mike hung for a few startled moments, limp as a kitten, before trying to wrench himself free.

"Not so fast!" his father growled, taking hold of Mike's upper arm. Mike had gone suddenly rigid as Luke's father marched him onto the porch. As they got closer, Luke saw that his father's fingers dug into the tender flesh just under Mike's armpit, pressing the nerve against the bone. His father's face was hard and angry. Mike's face was about to shatter.

Something landed gently on Luke's shoulder, feeling for a moment like a settling bird searching for balance on the branch of a tree. He glanced behind him and saw Mrs. Pederson peering at Mike, her clawlike hand perched on his shoulder.

Her face had undergone yet another transformation—Luke saw no gentleness, no humor, no kindness there. Hers was the face of a witch. Anger had fanned her black-seeming eyes to glowing coals. And hatred had scorched her white skin a livid red.

"And who are you?" she asked, her voice a flattened low note.

Mike was so scared that he couldn't get out his own name. He looked from Mrs. Pederson to Luke, his eyes begging for help. Luke stood, frozen in place, staring blankly at Mike, who began to cry.

Surprised, Luke's father let go of Mike's arm. Mike swallowed a sob and spun around, running down the sidewalk in a sloppy zigzag, as if he couldn't see straight.

"Well," his father said. "Maybe that'll teach him." He reached out and took Mrs. Pederson's elbow in his hand. "Are you all right, ma'am?"

Mrs. Pederson's mouth trembled and the fire in her eyes had turned to ash. She nodded and then whispered, "Let's go inside."

Silently, Luke followed his father and Mrs. Pederson into the house. They walked to the kitchen and sat around the table. Mrs. Pederson looked out the window and cleared her throat.

"Elijah and I owned an apple orchard . . . bought it after the war . . . a large orchard . . . where this part of town is now." Her voice sounded as if it were lost and she was struggling to find it. "Elijah set up the bell . . . that bell by the porch . . . for me to call him to dinner and . . . to call him in case of fire or tornado. I could always feel bad weather coming . . . in my bones. I could always tell when tornadoes or hail or blizzards were coming. He trusted my gift."

87

Luke breathed in, filling his lungs completely, and pictured the apple tree outside his bedroom window.

"The town grew," Mrs. Pederson continued. "And people began to steal apples as if the apples didn't belong to anybody . . . as if we didn't make our living from those apples. Once Elijah caught some boys selling apples . . . *our* apples . . . Jonathans . . . alongside the road. He boxed some ears and tanned some hides. And then the pranks started.

"The worst one was when the boys sneaked in and rang the bell. Each time Elijah came a-runnin', fearful that something was terribly wrong . . . that maybe I'd cut off my finger with a carving knife or that the chimney had caught fire. And when he found out he'd been tricked, he'd be madder than a wet cat. He'd fly into a rage."

Luke closed his eyes. The look on her face was ferocious—wounded and sad at the same time. With his eyes closed he seemed to feel her voice grow louder. He heard his father shifting his weight on his chair.

"One day I had a headache that grew until I thought my head would explode. I knew a bad storm was coming. I thought it might be a tornado. So, finally, when I couldn't stand it any longer, I rang the bell and Elijah came a-runnin'. He wanted to catch those boys red-handed as I rang and rang and he ran and ran, thinking it was those boys, and . . ." Mrs. Pederson breathed in sharply and Luke opened his eyes. Tears were streaking down her face and she began to sob.

"He dropped *dead* . . . heart attack . . . died when . . . his heart exploded . . . and . . . and his face was . . . *purple* and he was . . . *dead* . . . and his face lay in the mud and . . . and the tornado skipped over the house."

Luke shuddered and Mrs. Pederson covered her face with her hands. Luke's father stared out the window, his face set as hard as a piece of stone.

Luke heard her whisper through her hands. "The bell . . . it was the . . . the last thing he . . . he ever heard." She uncovered her mouth and her voice gathered strength. "I never, *never* wanted to hear that bell again until it rang to let Elijah know I was coming . . . coming on the wings of Death himself . . . coming to join him."

CHAPTER
10

Luke was glad to be back home from school, and alone. His mother wasn't home and his father was at his first day of community college. Carrying his math book to his bedroom, he lay down on his bed and looked out the window.

He stared at the old apple tree, whose branches reached out, almost touching his room. Since Mrs. Pederson had told of Elijah's death, he found himself staring at this tree often. Even though he'd looked at it all his life, during every season and in all kinds of light, he'd never known that it had once belonged to the Pedersons. Knowing that now made it look different and gave him the creeps.

But he didn't want to think about all that, and he closed his eyes, trying to relax, trying not to think of the rotten Monday he'd barely survived.

All day long, Mike got more and more on Luke's nerves. Mike was pissed and Luke didn't blame him. What had happened after Mike ran into his father had been awful. But Luke didn't think that Mike should be angry at him. *He* hadn't done anything to Mike. It hadn't been *his* fault.

If Mike had heard that story and seen Mrs. Pederson's face as she told it—if Mike hadn't been caught by Luke's father and felt humiliated by his father's treatment—if Luke's father hadn't called up Mike's parents and reported what Mike had done—if Mike hadn't rung the bell in the first place!—then Mike would have acted differently today.

But none of those *ifs* were true, and all day long Mike had made it impossible for Luke to tell him Mrs. Pederson's story. Mike had gone out of his way to be ornery, letting Luke know that he was no longer Luke's best friend. All day long Luke had tried to ignore Mike, hoping that everything would turn back to normal. But that had been next to impossible.

From the moment he got to school, Luke found that everywhere he turned Mike was there, staring at him with eyes made into slits that were almost as thin as his tight-lipped mouth. As hard as he tried, Luke couldn't get away from him. And every once in a while, when he least expected it, Mike would saunter up to him, muttering "I thought so" or "Weird" or "Cripes" as he walked by. And then, just when Luke was angry enough to bop him, Mike stopped. That was almost as annoying to Luke as his pestering.

Quietly, even though he was alone in the house, Luke got up from the bed, went to the window, unhooked the screen, and slipped outside. He wanted to leave his anger inside. Walking up to the apple tree, he turned and sat in the V made by two roots that were as thick as his thighs. He leaned back against the trunk and closed his eyes. Underneath his thighs and bottom he felt smaller roots that formed ropy webs between the larger roots. He tried to ignore the discomfort they caused. But it was as hard to ignore as Mike had been, and his anger at Mike's unfairness flared.

The way the roots felt merged with the trapped feeling he'd endured all day, and Luke flashed to the image of a tiger cage. He'd seen photographs in magazines—cubelike cages the Vietcong made of bamboo bars on all sides—barely big enough for an American prisoner-of-war to crouch inside. He wished he could stick Mike in one.

His eyes still closed, Luke pulled his legs under him and squatted. He pressed his elbows to his sides and imagined how Mike would feel, bound hand and foot, squatting on bamboo poles spaced several inches apart. Ropes looped around his neck, tying him to the top four corners of the bamboo cage. As he grimaced, his neck muscles tightened, and he pretended he was Mike, testing the ropes by leaning a little to his left and a little to his right.

He couldn't move far. When he moved left, the right ropes choked him. It was all so cleverly done that if Mike fell asleep, he would hang himself. And regardless of which direction he moved, the ropes were placed so that they tugged, disciplining him, making him stay perfectly, painfully still.

He wanted Mike to be in pain. And already, after just a few minutes in this make-believe tiger cage, Luke ached to move. He couldn't imagine how men lived for weeks, sometimes months, inside these boxes of torture. He wondered how long Mike would last. Two minutes, he decided—tops.

His neck ached from holding it in one position. Opening his eyes, he immediately wanted to melt into the ground.

His father stood off to his left, books under one arm, his sports jacket draped over the other, the knot of his tie pulled down, his shirt collar unbuttoned. He stared at Luke, puzzled.

Luke hoped his father hadn't figured out what he was doing under this tree. But if he had, he didn't let on. And then, to Luke's surprise, his father walked to the tree and sat one root over, grunting as he did so.

They didn't say anything for several minutes. Luke looked up as his father cleared his throat. "Had a hard day at school, too?" he asked.

Luke nodded. "Yeah," he said.

"I don't know." His father sighed, setting his books on his thighs and covering them with his jacket. "I just don't know. Guess I didn't remember how awful school can be . . . being cooped up in a classroom. I stand out like a sore thumb." He looked at Luke and Luke admired his father's clean-shaven face. "I don't have long hair and . . . Cripes! When I was a bricklayer . . . even at the end of a friggin' hot day . . . my clothes didn't stink like some of theirs do."

The question sprang from Luke's mouth, sounding to Luke like his mother when he got home from school. "What happened today . . . at school?"

His father looked at him, as if deciding whether or not he should tell him. "Well. I just . . . There were some things I heard today that . . ." He squinted at remembering. "Crud! They made me angry and I . . . I blew it. I mean, these two punks, they were sitting next to me and one of them—he had a beard—trying to look like Jesus Christ, for crissake! . . . was talking about the war and talking some garbage about American soldiers being war criminals. And this guy was talking that trash loud enough for me to hear. He goshdarn *wanted* me to hear! It was like I had a sign pinned to my backside that said: 'Vietnam Vet. Please kick!'"

Luke looked down from his father's face and saw his hands clasped on top of his jacket, the knuckles whitened. "He *wanted* me to hear," his father continued, his voice lower now. "He was baiting me and I almost acted like a large-mouthed bass . . . I almost took his bait. I almost knocked his friggin' head . . ."

The catch in his father's voice caused Luke to look up. His father was looking down at him, his eyes wide, as if he'd just realized something important. "What does he know, anyway! *Nothing*, that's what. I could've told him so much . . . about being there . . . about being in Vietnam. I could've told him how it *felt*. But, crud! He'd've just

94

laughed in my face. He wouldn't've understood squat."

Luke saw tears building in his father's eyes and suddenly, more than anything, he didn't want his father to cry. "He's just a hippie . . . you know, a draft dodger," he said, trying to sound brave but his voice coming out small and thin. In his hand he felt the Purple Heart and it startled him—he didn't remember putting his hand in his pocket.

His father nodded and kept looking at him. His Adam's apple bobbed as he swallowed. "I haven't known what to tell your mother . . . or you. There's so *much!* You just couldn't understand. Couldn't."

He glanced at Luke and saw Luke was staring at him. His eyes bounced away, shy and embarrassed. "Crud," he continued. "When I joined up, I knew it wasn't like World War Two. Now, *that* was a war *everybody* thought was right. Maybe in Vietnam it wasn't a *good* war, but it was *my* war . . . the war for *my* generation . . . and I didn't think it could be a bad war . . . not with President Johnson and everybody else over in Washington for it. Crud. I guess now I just didn't know *what* kind of war it was . . . in Vietnam."

Luke sensed his father's body relaxing as he talked. He noticed his fingers playing with the lapel of the sports jacket in his lap as he continued. "Did a lot of thinking in that hospital . . . in Tokyo . . . about why I joined, why I left you and your mother to go. I didn't have to join up but I . . .

I guess I was just cocky enough to think I was being a brave son-of-a-buck . . . like my old man in World War Two." He squinted, as if in pain. "Maybe some men are brave . . . better men than me, anyway. But the more I thought about it, the more I felt that I went over to that stinkin' hole because I *wasn't* brave . . . 'cause I told too many people what I thought about those protesters . . . 'cause I told too many people that those lousy creeps were *cowards* and that they didn't deserve to be Americans if they didn't lay it on the line . . . if they didn't fight for their country. Lord! It got so that I thought people would think *I* was a coward if I didn't go. . . ."

Luke tensed. He didn't want to hear what his father was saying. He didn't want it to be true.

"Everybody wants to be a hero . . . 'specially to their son . . . but I . . . I just don't want to lie to you, Luke. Not now." Luke didn't want to look at the pain he saw in his father's face, but he couldn't tear his eyes away. His father glanced down. "Luke, what're you fiddling with in your pocket?"

Luke's heart almost skipped a beat, and he looked down to where he held the Purple Heart. "Nothing," he mumbled.

"Come on, Luke. I ain't blind."

Slowly, fearfully, Luke pulled his hand out, and because the Purple Heart was pinned inside, the pocket came with it. Turning it palm side up, he uncurled his fingers. The Purple Heart lay in his hand, George Washington's face showing.

96

His father grunted. "It's a dandy, isn't it," he said. "But you know something, Luke? Nobody *wants* to get a Purple Heart. You don't go out of your *way* to get one. You have to get *wounded.*" Luke's fingers closed over the medal.

"Don't get me wrong," his father continued. "It was nice of them to give it to me, but it's not something that helps you remember anything . . . anything especially *wonderful.*"

And then his father began to laugh—a tense, unhappy laugh.

"You know where I was wounded?" His father's voice was sharp, had an angry edge to it.

Luke held his breath. Now that his father was going to tell him, he didn't know if he wanted to hear.

"Well, I'll tell you. My butt. My rear end. My *ass!* Couldn't sit for a month. Couldn't lie on my back. The bandages filled my pants like diapers, and that stinking cream they dressed it with stained my pants all the way through so that . . ." He leaned back against the tree. "That's not important," he said, closing his eyes and tipping his head back.

No! Luke cried inside. *No, no, no!* He didn't want to hear any more.

But his father continued. "We were on patrol . . . seven of us. We were supposed to be in a secured area so, as usual, we weren't being especially quiet . . . you know, we were horsing around. We knew better, but it felt so good to let off steam . . . you know? My buddy, Dick . . . Remember Dick? The one I wrote you about from New Mexico?"

97

He reached into his shirt from the top button and pulled out the dog tags. Fumbling with them for a moment, he held one out for Luke to see. "This one was Dick's."

Luke stared at the name punched with raised letters into the metal: Dick North. His father let the tags drop, and they landed on top of his tie. "Well, Dick was walking in front of me and was turning around to make some smart-ass joke. I heard something and the—" His father's head snapped toward Luke. "You sure you want to hear this?"

Stunned, Luke swallowed. He'd been wanting to know since he found out his father was wounded. Until now.

"I'm gonna tell you anyway," his father said, before Luke could answer. "I gotta." Tears welled up and he brushed them away angrily. "Dick was walking in front of me . . . and I heard something . . . a crack, maybe a stick breaking . . . maybe something else . . . and close, too . . . real close . . . and . . . and Dick's face disappeared. It just . . . just up and disappeared. There was *nothing* where his face had been. I mean, just a big . . . a *big* hole . . . and a sound came out and blood spurted and bubbled . . . like he was *trying* to say something only his mouth . . . his *face*, for crissake! . . . it wasn't there!" He was fighting his own breath, trying to keep from sobbing. "I dropped to the ground and I crawled around behind where Dick fell. I hid behind him and I . . . I listened to his last breath. Crud! And then they started firing at *me*. I tucked down and hid behind Dick . . .

98

like he was a bunch of sandbags or something . . . and I popped up every once in a while, my gun on rock'n'roll, firing over his chest. And I felt his body jerk every time a bullet hit him instead of me. And when everything got quiet, I felt something wet and I reached back and I grabbed . . . all I grabbed was a handful of . . . of blood and cloth . . . and . . ."

Luke stared at his father, his mouth open, his eyes wide, his heart beating in his throat. Tears poured down his father's face.

"I was . . . I was so *pissed* . . . *scared* . . . Hell, I'd messed my pants . . . right where I was shot . . . right in my wound. That's probably what caused the infection. And the guys used to joke around about diaper rash. . . ."

His father's face was slick. And the only thing Luke could think to do was to unpin the Purple Heart from his pocket and hold it out to his father. His fingers shook so hard, he pricked himself twice with the pin before he got it undone. His father's tears fell on the medal and on his hand for several minutes before he noticed what Luke was doing.

Taking the Purple Heart, his father said, "Crud!" Sniffling and trying to smile, he looked at Luke. "I'm sorry . . . I'm just a sorry ol' excuse for a father, Luke. I'm sorry. I *am!*"

And then he reached an arm around Luke's shoulder and pulled him close. Luke buried his face in his father's side and threw his arms around him, hugging as tightly as he could. He'd been longing to do this ever since his father had come home. He'd been longing so much it had hurt—he hadn't known how much until now.

And as he hugged his father, he fought his own tears. He fought and fought and fought.

But the tears won.

CHAPTER

11

Luke looked above the trees to the dark clouds that rose in the sky like a slow-motion wave about to break, about to crush the trees, about to crush him. Luke dawdled as he walked away from school. Occasional anger flashed through his body, as searing as lightning, and an aching disappointment grumbled in dark corners of his mind, wordless but as full of meaning as the strong, deep thunder coming from the clouds.

For the second day in a row, Mike had been ornery. Finally, at recess, when he couldn't take it anymore, Luke had walked up to Mike and stood in front of him, his hands on his hips, his elbows sharp and threatening.

"Hey, Mike," he'd said. "I'm sorry about my dad and all that . . . you know, at Mrs. Pederson's."

Mike had simply spun on his heel and stared in the opposite direction.

"Mike!" Luke pleaded. And Mike had walked away. Luke's face had wilted with the shock of Mike's meanness. His hands had slipped off his hips.

He looked at the dark clouds as he remembered

this, and he wished that Mike was with him and that he was Mike's sergeant. It was his turn to be sergeant, after all. He thought of all the painful, humiliating things he could order Mike to do.

I could tie him to a tree and hose him down and wait for lightning to strike him, he thought, looking once more at the ominous wall of cloud.

Or better yet, Luke thought, I could make him do knuckle pushups . . . in gravel.

And then he pictured Mike marching up and down the sidewalk in front of his house, wearing only his underwear. And Luke pictured kids from school gathering in his front yard staring and laughing and pointing at Mike. He grinned, thinking of how he would stand next to the sidewalk and wait until Mike marched by and then yank down the underpants.

Just as he was picturing Mike struggling to march with his knees banded together, Luke heard the slap-slap of footsteps approaching from behind. He looked over his shoulder just in time to see Mike whizz by.

"Hey, Mike," Luke called. "Mike!" But Mike kept on running as if he hadn't heard a thing.

And then it struck him. This wasn't even the way to Mike's house. Mike had run past his own house so that he could run past Luke and ignore him on purpose one more time.

Clenching his jaw to keep from yelling again, to keep from begging Mike to stop, Luke dropped his gaze and stared at the sidewalk. He felt a hot rush of tears in his eyes. But before they could spill, a circle of sidewalk cement instantly darkened and he heard a splat. And then another and another. Each darkened circle was the size of a quarter.

They weren't his tears—they came from the sky. Faster now, huge raindrops sizzled as they hit the sidewalk, inches apart, looking like bullet holes following Mike, striking closer and closer but never quite close enough, as Mike ran down the sidewalk and disappeared around a corner.

★

Luke couldn't believe it. His finger trembled as it reached toward the curled edge of the note taped to the refrigerator. Pencil scratches filled the piece of paper, the letters written in such haste that he could barely make out what they said: "At hospital with your mom. Go to Mike's. Will call later. Dad."

It was happening! His mother was having a baby.

He felt an incredible rush of happiness. And right behind the happiness came a jolt of fear. He'd heard that sometimes women died giving birth.

He stood facing the refrigerator, staring at the note, as these feelings collided in the middle of his chest. He gasped as the wave of happiness swallowed the fear and he let his math book drop to the kitchen floor. Jumping as high as he could, he punched the air with one fist and yelled, "Yahoo!"

He was suddenly so happy that he felt as if

somebody had pumped him full of the wonderful news. "All right!" he bellowed, using one whole breath. But as much happiness as he let out, even more rushed in to take its place.

And then he thought of Mike. It was as if he'd been punctured. His father wanted him to go to Mike's house. He was going to call at Mike's house. But that was the last place in the world Luke wanted to go. So, what if his father couldn't get him there? He'll call here, Luke reasoned.

Glancing at the window, he saw it had begun to rain fitfully. The rain made his decision to stay home feel even more right.

And then he thought of Mrs. Pederson. "Crud!" he muttered. Mrs. Pederson was expecting him to help her this afternoon—had even paid him a little something in advance and then told him not to tell his father—that his father might not approve of his being paid at all for work that was supposed to be a punishment. But even with the money, Luke couldn't help her. Not now, not if his father was going to call at any minute from the hospital. Even so, he didn't feel right about not showing up. He wished she had a telephone.

It won't take long, he told himself, and he charged toward the door.

The rain had stopped, and the dark polka dots on the cement were fading as they dried, filling the air with the ripe smell of rain. He ran toward Mrs. Pederson's, so full of his news that it took him a half block for the silence to hit him.

He stumbled to a stop and looked around him, straining to hear. He heard nothing. It was as if

104

he'd gone deaf. No birds sang. No wind rustled the leaves of the trees. No dogs barked. With relief, he heard the distant sound of a car.

And then, as his ears strained to hear anything more—it came to him, almost floating, as soft as a bubble popping.

He heard the sound of the bell ringing. The sound grew in his mind—a long-forgotten memory rising to the surface.

It was Mrs. Pederson's bell.

Why?

And the wind answered him with a roar, sounding like an enormous wave ready to crest, ready to smash into the top of the clouds and fall, churning, on top of him.

And then the sirens started to wail.

He began to run just as the wind struck, smacking his face like a swung pillow, knocking him off balance. The sound of the bell was drowned in the shrill of the wind. *She must feel it in her bones.* He ran toward Mrs. Pederson's house, butting his head against the wind.

Rain began to fall, stinging. The wind pulled the breath out of him and he struggled to hold some inside.

His only thought was of Mrs. Pederson. He pictured her standing by her bell, buffeted by the wind, holding on to the rope for balance as she rang the bell, her dress blowing behind her, shredding as it flapped.

A page of newspaper, held down on the sidewalk by the wind, leaped up. It pounced on Luke's face, pressing hard. Luke tore at it, ripping off hunks of paper, feeling as if he were tearing off hunks of his own skin.

Picking up his pace, he ran with only one thought in mind—that he had to get to Mrs. Pederson because she'd been calling for help.

The hedge loomed, the branches thrashing. Sand blasted his face and he ran through the gap in the hedge and into Mrs. Pederson's yard.

The wind continued to shriek, but its force was diminished. Luke grew dizzy in the relative stillness, as if he were floating round and round in an eddy of water. As he ran from the hedge, the eddy grew more powerful, swirling like flushed water—pulling him— sucking him— toward the porch. He looked up, expecting to see a funnel searching for him with its hoselike mouth. Instead, he saw shredded bits of blackened cloud and the shingles of Mrs. Pederson's house raised like the hair of a frightened cat.

Luke staggered up the steps and threw open the screen door and pushed his way inside. The house shuddered and he threw his weight backwards against the door, forcing it shut.

Turning around, looking down the throat of the hallway, he saw Mrs. Pederson standing, hugging her own shoulders, her face like that of a ghost. Her eyes were closed and she rocked back and forth, as if trying to comfort herself. "I'm coming, Elijah!" she wailed. "I'm a-coming!"

"Mrs. Pederson!" he yelled. She opened her eyes and her mouth. She struggled to loosen her own grip on her shoulders and held out her arms to him. She looked like a terrified child.

He ran to her and grabbed both of her hands before she could throw her arms around him. He ran under her arms, pulling her toward the kitchen. She followed, as if they were part of an insane square dance, tugging at him so lightly that he felt he must be dragging a flag that was fluttering in a light breeze.

He spied the darkness under the table and stopped. Seeing fear in Mrs. Pederson's eyes, he tried to sound reassuring even as he yelled loudly enough to be heard. "Mrs. Pederson! Under there! We'll be safe . . . under there!"

Closing her mouth, she nodded and lowered herself stiffly to her knees and crawled underneath. He followed, and she huddled next to him and against the wall, which pulsed with the force of the wind that was beating against the house.

Luke reached for a chair, toppling it as he pulled it under the table. It lay sideways, a barrier against attack. He grabbed the other two chairs around the table for protection, making walls of the chairbacks and legs. He knew the chairs wouldn't do much against the storm's fury, but it was better than nothing.

He looked at Mrs. Pederson. Incredibly, her knees were drawn up to her chest and she stared at him, forlorn and lost, pitiful and small. Leaning toward her, he reached around her shoulder and held her close, as if she were a child and he were the father. He wished he could whisper to her, tell her that everything was going to be all right. But the wind never took a breath, never let up in its howling. All he heard mixed in with the wind was the faint, musical sound of a window exploding.

Suddenly it was deafeningly silent, so silent it was hard to breathe, as if the wind had snatched away the air as well as sound.

As the silence hit, Mrs. Pederson began to shiver so hard he thought that she would fly apart.

Luke scrambled over a huge branch that lay across the sidewalk, torn from a large elm tree during the storm. The walk was littered with debris—shingles and shredded leaves piled up against bushes and fences and bits of greasy paper and foil that had blown from tipped-over garbage cans.

Mike saw the jockey shorts first, lying in the middle of the sidewalk. Luke was surprised they were there—most everything of value had been picked up by now. Running to them, Mike plucked them off the cement as if they were soiled and grinned at Luke. "I wonder who lost these?"

Luke laughed, picturing a naked boy running around town, searching for the underwear that had been blown right off his body. "We'll know him when we see him," Luke said.

Mike dropped the shorts and scrambled over the crooked elbow of an arm-shaped branch, excited now about finding other treasures.

Luke was happy to be friends with Mike again. The day his baby sister had come home, Mike had come over to see her. Mike had acted as if nothing had happened between them, and Luke took that for an apology.

Looking around from where he stood, Luke found it was tempting to think that what he saw was the result of an enemy bombing raid. It was tempting to think of enemy bombers in formation, flying so low that you could almost see the pilots behind their glass bubbles—to imagine taking aim at these planes with a machine gun and riddling their sleek, fishlike underbellies with bullets, bringing them down in flames.

For five days now, the town had been a perfect place to play war, to imagine attacks and counterattacks. A couple of houses had lost their roofs, and most houses had at least one or two boarded-up windows. A few cars, looking like smashed bugs, remained parked alongside curbs, the trees or utility poles that had rested on top of them gone now. Large trees that had tipped over left craters where their roots had grown. From the right angle these craters looked as if they'd been created by mortar, lobbed into town from nearby cornfields.

Mike and Luke had played hard the past couple of days, using the destruction caused by the tornado as the most realistic battlefield on which they'd ever played. They had played so hard at war that, much to their amazement, they were all played out for now.

Mike's head popped up from behind the branch where he'd been stooped over, looking. He smiled. "Well, have you changed her diapers yet?"

"Sure," Luke said, even though he hadn't. He'd held his sister, Catherine, and watched her sleep. But that was about all. He couldn't say she was cute, but he found himself studying her, his eyes tracing the folds of skin on her face—especially under her chin and around her eyes. And he'd felt her fingers, which seemed so delicate that he was afraid they might snap off. When she'd grabbed one of his fingers, he was shocked at how strong her grip was.

"Pretty gross, huh?" Mike said. "Like great big gobs of greasy grimy gopher guts, huh?"

Instead of answering, instead of pretending that he knew, Luke leaned forward and shouted, "Race you!" And he started running, dodging garbage that still lay on the sidewalk.

He heard Mike close behind him and tried to speed up, but there was too much stuff in his way. Not wanting Mike to hear how hard he was working, he forced himself to breathe through his nose. His nostrils drew air as well as a flattened straw.

And then Mike passed him.

"Hey!" Luke cried out, as if Mike were cheating.

He tried to catch up but just couldn't. Mike's driveway was right ahead and he kept his eyes on it, disappointed when Mike reached it first.

"Want to come in . . . watch something on TV?" Mike asked, trying to keep from panting. His chest heaved anyway and Luke was glad that Mike had to work plenty hard to beat him.

"Can't . . . gotta get home," Luke said. "Want to come over to see the baby?"

"Naw." Mike screwed up his face, as if disgusted. "I've already seen her once. Seen one baby, you've seen them all."

"Want to help me at Mrs. Pederson's later?" Luke asked. Yesterday both he and Mike had worked for her, cleaning up the yard from the storm. And trimming the hedge.

"Aw, I don't know." Mike looked down at his feet, tapping his right foot, the toe of his shoe fanning back and forth in an arc. Mrs. Pederson paid them hardly anything at all for their work. Luke didn't mind so much—he still felt guilty about the trouble he'd caused her. But Mike had been so disappointed that he'd barely remembered to thank her.

"Well, if you want to, I'll be there."

Mike looked up, his eyes sheepish. "Okay. I might," he said. "Or I might not." And then he laughed, turned, and walked up his driveway, waving a hand without bothering to turn around.

"See you tomorrow," Luke called after him.

Luke was careful going into the house, trying not to make any noise. Tiptoeing through the kitchen, he listened for telltale sounds of Catherine. He heard nothing but the drip-drip of the kitchen faucet.

Walking into the living room, he saw his mother lying on the sofa. Her bare feet poked out

112

from a wildly colored crocheted afghan that was pulled up to her shoulders. Her eyes were closed, and Luke saw bumps under the afghan that made him think that her hands held each other, resting below her gently rising and falling chest—where her stomach had been so large only a few days before.

Since she had come back from the hospital, Luke had found himself looking at her as if something were wrong. He remembered how funny he had thought she looked with her beach-ball belly. But now she looked funny without it—flat and shrunken. Holding his breath to be extra quiet, Luke walked to the bedroom hallway. If his mother was asleep in the living room without Catherine, Luke knew that his father must be home from school and in their bedroom.

Luke sniffed. The house smelled more complicated these days. The air was heavy with the scent of curdled milk, sweetened. And mixed in was the smell of baby powder and a faint sourness that was strongest in the bathroom, where the diaper pail sat next to the stool.

Hesitating, Luke peeked inside his parents' bedroom. In the middle of the bed was Catherine, in a cocoon of pink baby blankets. On the edge of the bed sat his father, gazing down at the baby. His father looked tired, but not in the same way he'd looked when he'd come home from Vietnam. He looked tired and happy at the same time—as if he'd run a long race and won.

Luke stood for several minutes, until his father sensed he wasn't alone with Catherine and

113

looked up. "Howdy," his father whispered, smiling. Quietly, Luke crossed over to his parents' bed and sat on the edge opposite his father. Leaning over, he peered into Catherine's face. She wasn't looking as puffy and red as she had been looking this morning. But he still couldn't decide if she looked more like his father or more like his mother. Or like him.

As he watched, Catherine's mouth moved and her eyes closed tighter and she sighed, a bubble of spit appearing in the corner of her mouth. And then she gave out a little squeak and her eyes opened a crack. Her mouth was closed but her jaws began to work, and suddenly her mouth gaped and she began to cry. For such a tiny thing she made a very large sound.

His father sighed. "Crud. I was afraid that would happen . . . while your mom was resting," he said, loud enough to be heard above Catherine's cry. "Time for another feeding, most likely. We'll just have to wake up your mother."

"No need to do that."

Luke and his father looked toward the bedroom door. There stood Luke's mother, her hair rumpled and her face tired, but her smile charged with energy, her cheeks fairly glowing.

"I swear I heard her cry in my head before she opened her mouth," she said, walking to the bed.

Luke's mother stared at Catherine as if she couldn't believe what she was seeing. And then she sat next to Luke's father and began pulling up the tails of her blouse and unbuttoning it at the same time. Luke knew there was nothing bad

114

about Catherine sucking on his mother's breasts. But yesterday when he'd seen his mother take out a breast and offer it to Catherine, he'd felt giggly nervous, as if he'd walked in on his mother while she was taking a bath. He'd also felt jealous, wanting to be close to his mother, to be cradled that way in her arms. And he'd felt curious, wondering how it all worked—the breast and the sucking and the milk.

He knew his mother didn't mind his being there. But it all seemed private—something just between his mother and Catherine. Before his mother finished unbuttoning her blouse, Luke turned his head and got to his feet. The crying stopped as suddenly as it had started. "Gotta help Mrs. Pederson for a while," he said.

His father cleared his throat. "I'll walk you there, maybe see what you've been working at so hard."

"I'll see you two later." Luke stole a glance at his mother as he walked out of the bedroom. She held Catherine against her opened blouse and her eyes were partly closed. She looked as if she were listening to the most beautiful music in the world.

Luke and his father walked through the house in silence. As they stepped outside, Luke's father paused for a moment and threw his head back, letting the sunlight smack him in the face. "Isn't this the berries!" he said, smiling. And then he looked down at Luke. "Makes *me* feel like a fifth wheel too, Luke. But isn't it a pretty sight, your mother feeding Catherine like that?"

115

Luke scuffed at the pavement with the toe of his right foot. "Yeah," he said, looking up and trying to smile. The smile came easier than he'd thought it would.

"Just like you used to do," his father added. Luke felt himself blushing.

His father held out a hand, and Luke looked at it for a moment. He couldn't remember the last time he'd held his father's hand. He felt too old for it but he didn't want to hurt his father's feelings—and the hand was tempting. Slipping his hand into his father's, he was surprised at how comfortable it felt as they walked down the driveway and turned onto the sidewalk. He liked the way his father's thumb stroked his knuckles and the backs of his fingers.

"Don't think I told you how proud I am of how you helped Mrs. Pederson the other day . . . during the storm." His father squeezed Luke's hand and let it go.

Luke looked down to hide his embarrassed smile. "I had to let her know and then . . ."

"Luke, I've been thinking . . . just a little bit and . . ." His father frowned. "What you did took courage . . . the kind of courage I saw a lot of in Vietnam. Now, I bet you anything you didn't get up that morning and say to yourself, 'I'm gonna act courageous today. Gonna do something to make 'em proud.'" He smiled. "You just did what you *had* to do, *when* you had to do it. Like helping her during the storm . . . and helping her now. *That's* courage, Luke. I don't know anything else that says it better ... except what your ma went through at the hospital."

Luke ached with things that he wanted to say but that didn't have words. "Dad," he said quietly, trying anyway, "I'm sorry ... about everything."

They turned a corner and Mrs. Pederson's hedge came into view. One flank of it was wild and shaggy, going off to their left. Running straight down the sidewalk away from them, the other flank was neat as a brick wall—at least as high as Luke could reach with the hedge trimmers.

"Looks like you could use a little help with the top there," his father said, stopping.

"Yeah." Luke had thought of borrowing somebody's ladder to help with the high parts.

His father cleared his throat. "Since everybody's apologizing all over the place ... well, Luke, I've been wanting to do some apologizing myself ... to you. I'm ... I'm sorry about ... about everything too and ..." His eyebrows knocked together. "Crud!" he muttered and then smiled, reaching into his pocket.

Luke stared as his father handed him the Purple Heart.

"Here," his father said. "I'd be proud for you to help take care of this thing for me. You've earned it, what with the way I've been acting and all."

Luke took the medal with trembling fingers. George Washington looked off to the left, calm and unflustered, as he closed his hand over it.

"Thanks," he said, not trusting his voice to say

117

anything more. And then he pinned it on his shirt.

His father placed a hand on Luke's shoulder and squeezed it gently.

AUTHOR'S NOTE

On August 7, 1782, General George Washington established the first American military decoration. Called the Badge of Military Merit, it was made of purple cloth cut into the shape of a heart and edged with narrow lace. "The road to glory in a patriot army and a free country is opened to all," General Washington wrote, making it clear that this military decoration was to be the first ever awarded to deserving officers and enlisted men without regard to their rank. It soon became known as the Purple Heart. Nobody knows for certain why General Washington chose the shape of a heart or the color purple—but today it seems a perfect symbol of bravery while under fire.

Only three people are known to have been awarded General Washington's Badge of Military Merit. The first was Sergeant Elijah Churchill of the Fourth Troop, Second Regiment of Light Dragoons, for his gallantry, extraordinary fidelity, and essential service in the raids of Fort St. George on November 23, 1780, and Fort Slongo on October 2, 1781. After the Revolutionary War the decoration fell into disuse and was almost forgotten for one hundred fifty years.

In 1932, in part to commemorate the two hundredth anniversary of George Washington's birth (February 22, 1732), General Douglas MacArthur revived the Badge of Military Merit as an Army decoration to be officially called the Purple Heart Medal. It soon became the only military decoration to recognize soldiers in the Army who suffered wounds, injuries, or death while in combat action against an enemy of the United States.

In 1942 President Roosevelt extended the Purple Heart to members of the Navy, Marine Corps, and Coast Guard. In 1952 President Truman made the Purple Heart retroactive to April 5, 1917, which allowed World War One servicemen to receive the medal. In 1962 President Kennedy extended eligibility for the Purple Heart to any American civilian who served with a branch of the armed forces.